cash 4 gold

BOY

a novel

PETER VACK

Cash 4 Gold Books

www.c4gbooks.com

ISBN: 979-8-9907275-1-9

Cover artwork: Peter Vack
Cover layout: Chris Habib
Book design: Tex Gresham

PROLOGUE

If only he could remove his skin. Unzip, step out, and replace it with something more fashionable—cashmere, fleece, cured meat (prosciutto)—anything but his perfect microscopic pores. Sillyboy knows his accomplishments do not yet warrant heroic suicide: a luxury afforded tortured geniuses or abject failures, not almost male-starlets like Sillyboy. Also, it would make his parents too upset and reveal an embarrassing amount of anger. He is 28 and if he could adopt any quality from his phone, it would be its fluid relationship with mortality. Maybe one day someone will invent a plug for Sillyboy.

Chloe doesn't know how to bring up the subject of Sillyboy's Instagram. A white person is not allowed to post photos of Black people without eyes; or burn victims; or amputees with 3D-printed limbs; or photos of Al-Qaeda beheadings cropped and edited to conceal the gore.

When he was younger, Sillyboy prayed every night to the capitalist deity to transform his adolescent acne to adult beauty.

"Make me beautiful. Make me beautiful. Please dear God, do me this solid, and make me beautiful," Sillyboy would chant in front of his mirror, massaging his jawline and squeezing his zits. "I can't succeed without beauty and, if I do, I don't want it. I need to look at myself and see a successful, happy, and undeniably handsome man."

What a tragic outcome for Sillyboy to live and succeed without the face of a God.

Is it misogynistic to nickname an emotional outburst a "titty-fit?" Sillyboy thinks it is but doesn't want to press the issue. Chloe hates feminism and feminists as many girls her age do. As many men his age are, Sillyboy is terrified of feminism and feminists.

A wave of anxiety crashes around him. He must soon sit at his computer and forge meaning and value from his life. (Sillyboy is not actually silly. Sillyboy is white. White guilt is about to go mainstream in America. In the future, I will be known as a white guilt influencer. I am a trend forecasting savant. An author I admire posted "trendiness is one of the worst qualities in an author." There are so many people I want to impress online. There are so many voices influencing mine. I want to be provocative, but I am conflicted. Before publishing, I must go through the manuscript and redact the slurs.)

Sillyboy wants to travel to the future to experience his life as a finished product; a long Wikipedia article linking Sillyboy and his prolific output to all the crucial players of his time.

But that is impossible and corny.

•

    Sillyboy enters his parents' apartment overcome by happiness. He finds them sitting on a small balcony overlooking the East River eating bowls of puffed millet, raw almonds, chia seeds, sunflower seeds, shredded coconut, flax seeds, blueberries, and banana made moist with coconut water; good for the colon and blood, another weapon in the ongoing battle to preemptively combat illness and live a century with functioning bodies and brains. Sillyboy is telling his parents something so fascinating they can't take their eyes off him. They hang on his every word, sparkling with admiration and pride. This is their boy, he is so smart, anything he ever wanted he received and yet he isn't spoiled. It's a miracle, it's fantastic! How we reared such an excellent, mature, and loving young man, we aren't quite sure. Well, perhaps it has something to do with the tremendous amount of work we have done as parents— reading, therapy, reading, therapy, reading, group therapy, and reading coupled with constant careful conscious living, packed and loaded with deep analytical reflection; yes, it must have something to do with the way he was raised. Okay, sure, we can take credit where credit is due; we can own up to our achievement without allowing it to bloat our perspective. A moment or two of self-congratulation is allowed every once in a while. It was our ambition in life to be the best parents, and we did it! We did it! We did! Look at our boy, our beautiful son! Look at our intelligent boy! Look at our boy, wise beyond his years! Look at our boy, talented! Look at our boy, walking with great determination, and carefully, step by step—little by little as we always advised—down the long road towards happiness, health, and so much success! Look at our boy, Sillyboy! Look at our adorable Sillyboy; and, of course, we're aware one's exterior is secondary, and on this we don't want to dwell, but he is just so handsome, a statue, hunky and, dare we say, hot? We know our audience—we wouldn't gush like this to just anyone; we wouldn't, but in this moment, everyone—knock on wood—full of happiness and health, it feels appropriate to bask in the glory of our young man, our greatest accomplishment, our son, our precious, precocious, brilliant Godhead son.

ONE

"How you want me to spell that?"
"Oh, um, S…I…L…L…"
"Hold up. Hold up. Lemme get a pen."

His eyes drift down to the floor, epoxy the color of asphalt, as a small quantity of booze flavored acid belches to the back of his throat. He hates drinking. He hates people who drink. Last night, at a bar filled with gays in Hawaiian shirts, Sillyboy, a lime-green Lei draped around his neck, got drunk on two tequilas while waiting for his ex to arrive, furious to be stood up while acknowledging it was also totally like her.

Now, Sillyboy is standing in front of a full-length mirror. The tattooer returns with a ballpoint pen to get the spelling correct before stenciling the tattoo on Sillyboy's stomach in orange Sharpie. Sillyboy is getting his name tattooed over his bellybutton with a stylish new spelling.

"How you spell that again?"
"S…I…L…L…Y…B…O…I."

The oscillating needle of the tattoo machine connects with his flesh and the sensation is not the agony he expected. Needles hurt, but a tattoo is an ambiguous discomfort like cheap pharmacy socks with the seam stitched right at the toes. Once the tattoo is finished, it is more beautiful than Sillyboi could have imagined. He takes a photograph of his stomach, swollen and bloody, and texts it to Chloe who responds:

Wowowowow only the best for my baby!! Followed by an ecstatic string of emojis.

•

Sillyboi walks down a wide anonymous stretch of the San Fernando Valley past a dilapidated strip mall—decaying signage dripping from vacant storefronts—Robeks, 7-Eleven, and a taco cart. Tomorrow, he returns to New York City. His cellphone buzzes with a call from his ex. He hopes she is calling to apologize. He lets it buzz to voicemail.

In Los Angeles, every walk leads to a parking space. Sillyboi sees his rental car in the distance and prays he survives the drive to his hotel.

His ex calls again. Her contact is still saved as "Ms. Slow Death." Either he can listen to her explanation or punish her. He chooses the latter and feels guilty.

Depending on the temperament of the Gods, the freeway can either be a long serpentine strip of parking lot or miraculously empty. Today, the Gods smiled on Sillyboi's journey from the valley to the Dream Hotel in Hollywood, where he is now, relaxing on a hard little couch staring at

Charlize Theron looming outside his window, forehead and eyes streaked with black oil riding shotgun next to a muzzled Tom Hardy, in a billboard for Mad Max: Fury Road. His phone vibrates with a text.

Did you get my voicemail?

Sillyboi listens:

"Hey, so, um, yeah," Ms. Slow Death's tone is unpredictable with whines of irony and throbs of candor. "Sorry I didn't show up last night. I get that that was uncool of me. But I just couldn't come. Are you leaving tomorrow? I'd still like to see you. Could you come to me later? I'm in Los Feliz. Um, yeah, let me know and I'll give you the address, if you don't have it, which, I think you should actually."

Sillyboi already agreed to eat a late lunch with his best friend Ivan. Ivan shaves his chest and wears a gray tank top and blue swim trunks. Fake Wayfarers with pink temples hold his thick brown hair off his high forehead. Ivan takes a small sip from a tall glass and pops a piece of spicy tuna roll in his mouth. Sillyboi is hunched over his seaweed salad like a beggar. Behind them, across the street, is an auto body shop clogged with mechanics on strike wielding signs and bullhorns around a big inflatable rat: fangs out, ready to kill, but slowly deflating.

"I am so happy these days." Ivan says.

"That's incredible."

A couple of strikers argue near a hole in the rat's tail.

"Are you good, you seem good, you look gorgeous.

Your skin is perfect like beautiful white stone." Ivan takes the last piece of sushi to his mouth. Sillyboi is thankful to have Ivan in his life. To have someone other than his mother, father, and his gf Chloe who recognizes his beauty. Sillyboi laughs away the compliment.

"It's so good to see you, Sillyboy. I miss you in New York. How is it there?"

"It's good, like, I prefer it, but you know…" What Sillyboi would like to say is this: "Ivan, help me, I am stuck in my dependency. I am still most comfortable in my parents' house, lounging on their balcony and looking out at the Manhattan skyline, indulging in our blissful conversations about me, about my career, about the future, about anything. How is it, as I approach thirty, my mother and my father are still my best friends? How is it we have only ever seen eye-to-eye and my intentions have only been to make them proud and uphold my reputation as their perfect little boy who only does right, who only makes them proud, who accomplishes what he sets out to do, and keeps his micro-rebellions far away and out of sight?" *We are counting the days,* Sillyboi thinks, *counting the days till disaster strikes and our family will be forced to suffer the indignity of one of life's random tragedies. Cells quietly mutating as another conflict-free day passes. The humbling no happy family can avoid.*

But Sillyboi cannot share this with Ivan. Happy Ivan, oblivious to the strikers throwing up their hands and sopping with sweat, as their mascot deflates.

"I am making art right now," Ivan says. "Every day, I wake up, I make the decision to stay sober, and I produce an important piece of art."

"I've seen the videos. They're hysterical. They're literally perfect."

"Oh, Sillyboy that's... thank you, you know how important your support is to me."

"I'm basically in awe and jealous of how prolific you are."

"Have we talked about...shut me up if we have, but have we—"

"What?"

Ivan takes a breath.

"I've realized, somewhat recently, I am actually a genius."

Sillyboi nods for Ivan to continue, praying his explanation of "genius" is relatable.

"And I can use this genius," Ivan continues, "it doesn't have to be something I'm ashamed of, or that I question, it can just be the engine of my work. And my work can be plentiful. I'm having fun making sketches go viral on YouTube but soon it will be TV shows, movies, franchises of movies that can be turned into, like, action figures and theme parks. I can move people. It's like, I used to see what I wanted as this thing." Ivan grazes his fingertips across his chest, from sternum to shoulders, becoming even broader and more erect. "Like, I always knew I could, if I wanted to. Be on the level of the greats, but, anytime I ever tried to translate this feeling into something concrete, in an actual professional setting, my anxiety destroyed me. I would just see myself as this scared guy from Kentucky with chubby cheeks who wasn't valuable enough to stand in a shitty casting room in L.A. And, I guess it had something to do with booking the CBS diversity showcase because, after that, something in me just … I finally realized I am deeply funny. There's nothing I have to change about myself to accomplish being funny. It's entwined in the fabric of my being. I am funny. That is just a fact about me. I am professionally funny. Whenever I want. I can be funny. I can be funny in front of whoever I want. I am a character actor. I am also profoundly handsome and beautiful. I understand this now. And, of course, as I am saying this, I feel a bit flooded by critical thoughts that, like, I should be self-conscious or modest or something. But I can just as easily see these thoughts as nothing. They aren't real. They're fantasy. A fantasy of an older self, straightjacketed by fear and self-loathing, which is also fear."

"That sounds really positive Ivan. I am really happy for you."

"I am a genius. You are also a genius, Sillyboy. I wouldn't be saying this to you if I didn't feel we were on the same level. I am not afraid anymore. I am fearless. An idea comes for a video and I make it. It's as simple as that."

"The one about the pre-brunch ritual was inspired."

"It has three-and-a-half-million views."

"Wow."

"It's not even my favorite. But I'm proud of it. Thank you, yes, it's great. But prouder than any video, I am proud of my output and the confidence I have to stand in my power and be the artist, the brilliant artist, I am. I wake up every morning with this deep intuition I am on the right path and my work is the future."

Sillyboi came to LA, got a tattoo, and changed the spelling of his name—the conventional "y" that cannot help but exist in a perpetual state of questioning "Y, Y, Why," replaced with the daring "I," the fuck-you "I," the "I" that proclaims his new identity, his "I, I, I!"—but as bold as these actions were, they did nothing to produce the passionate self-love and confidence Sillyboi sees on full display in Ivan. Sillyboi is desperate to show Ivan his new tattoo and reveal his brave new self to his old best friend but, overcome by anxiety, he decides to stay hidden.

"I couldn't agree with you more." Sillyboi says.

They walk to Ivan's car, a dilapidated white Corolla—the only one Ivan could afford after totaling his previous newer beige Corolla on the occasion of his third DUI—and the sun dissects into many subsidiary beams, piercing the smog to produce a feeling that alludes to a relaxation that is total and lifelong.

Sillyboi hugs Ivan goodbye.

"I really appreciate you." Ivan says.

"I really appreciate you." Sillyboi replies.

TWO

Driving to meet Ms. Slow Death, Sillyboi has trouble remembering the personality he used when they were a couple. Did they share inside jokes? When Sillyboi thinks of the voice he used, he can feel his vocal cords constrict with too much sarcasm. *But I was funny once or twice.* Sillyboi thinks. The sex was bad. Sillyboi could not maintain his erection. There were times when they read the paper side-by-side and pretended they were smart. So a clearer picture is forming of their relationship; it was a little funny, a little smart, and not at all sexy.

A year ago, around the time Sillyboi and Ms. Slow Death broke up, his attention was co-opted by the stream of images on Instagram. Now, every morning upon waking, he brings his phone to his face to transmit soothing square images: tattoos, goth girls in necklaces, massive asses, washboard abs, memes, airbrushed skin, average friends attempting to look extraordinary, and the ubiquity of food. Ms. Slow Death has a private account and Sillyboi wouldn't dare risk the anxiety of a request, so her image is absent from his feed, her face receded into memory, diminished by weed and offloaded to his phone and the hard drives piling up around his desk.

He is doing his best not to smoke weed, but everywhere he goes he can smell it. On every street corner an old man is rolling a joint; beckoning him—come, have a puff, Silly, come sit by Grandpa and enjoy the last pinch of cannabis on earth.

Sillyboi stops at a red light and lifts his shirt to inspect the intricate lettering. *So cool,* thinks Sillyboi. *So radical and so cool. I am tattooed. For life. A punk. A rebel. Fuck it, I'm an artist! Like Ivan, this proclaims my genius! My undeniable me-ness! It authenticates me. I look at this marking and I know I have an obligation to my art and to myself! And it's cool. So cool. Of course, that's important. Its coolness. Finally, cool. Finally, I can say I give no fucks. A beautiful lack of fucks led me out of New York, thousands of miles from my parents and their smothering love, overwhelming support, to a tattoo shop in Van Nuys to be changed forever. Yes! I am cool! I am on Instagram, and I am tattooed, and I am exactly as a person under thirty should be in 2015, cool and without a fuck to give.*

Sillyboi resumes driving as his thoughts veer away from Ms. Slow Death and towards Celeste.

"Why is everyone always talking about themselves?" is the question Sillyboi associates with Celeste, both of them rolling on molly at a wrap party for an independent film. The question is obvious, but Sillyboi often asks the same one. They were alone in a Long Island parking lot surrounded by cars, apart from the others, super-high, talking about nothing. Were it not for his gf Chloe at home, Sillyboi would have already made his move, but playing the part of good boy, he is listening and gritting, listening and gritting to will away the influence of his influential cock.

But the trouble with Sillyboi is that he doesn't actually listen. He thinks he listens—intently, patiently, his furrowed brow is presented to the jury as evidence—and when listing his good qualities, Sillyboi would count his ability as a listener as high on that list. But what if Sillyboi has made a grave error in his self-appraisal, and it is actually others who are always listening to him? Sillyboi has enjoyed so many hours of being deliciously received by others and, as a result, is so familiar with the experience of being received, with patient looks of attentiveness from his family, friends, and girlfriend—his audience—that somewhere in the course of his life, the constant passionate reception of his every thought and feeling, his minor emotional flatulence taken for grave philosophical pronouncement, Sillyboi began to mistake the experience of being listened to for the act of listening itself.

This is the moment of transgression. Watch closely or else you might miss it. Sillyboi—still Sillyboy, before the tattoo—is an actor. Celeste is an actress. In the film, Sillyboy and Celeste played a couple who mistake their lust for love. Celeste walked Sillyboy to a secluded area between parked cars. Sillyboy's fantasy is simple: he fucks Celeste, tastes her cunt, and becomes intoxicated by the otherness of her body. Sadly, the otherness of Chloe, as cute and sexy as a girl can be, is starting to wane; her allure still potent, but diminished by the gallon of semen—or two, or three, or four, or five—

he has injected inside her. And Celeste's fantasy? Well, Sillyboy cannot guess what might be motivating Celeste to make sure they are alone together. Sillyboy had been trying to listen to Celeste all night; so much so, he couldn't remember a single word she said.

Celeste sat on a strip of pavement between cars and rolled her head on her neck making small half circles with her chin. *This is the moment I would make my move,* Sillyboy thought, as a pool of saliva formed in his mouth and the chemical serpent, introduced by the drugs, undulated in his jaw.

"Why are people always talking about themselves?" Celeste said, and, with that innocent question, so begins their transgression. Celeste on the ground, sliding back and forth on her enormous behind. Sillyboy over her, tempted to give in to desire, to drugs, to confirm the lowest expectations of his sex. Celeste's tongue across the front of her teeth. Sillyboy panting like a dog, painting a portrait of lust on his face. Her legs. Her pert tits. Her slice of midriff. Sillyboy makes a great show of looking, and yet, no parts touch.

There it was. Don't claim to have missed it. The first moment of transgression. Sillyboy, not even close to Celeste but imagining them fucking, made quiet grunting noises. Celeste talked and talked like nothing was happening and no one was listening.

•

Sillyboi is minutes away from Ms. Slow Death's apartment and he still can't remember the voice he used when they were in love. *What a shame it is,* Sillyboi thinks, *to forget a former self*. Sillyboi knows Ms. Slow Death loved the old him and suspects the voice he once used was smarter, wittier, and more of a feminist.

Sillyboi parks in an open space directly in front of a squat pale pink apartment complex and walks the hundred steps it takes to transport his body from the car to her door, behind which he imagines she has just poured herself a glass of sauvignon blanc and is settling down to read one of the many screenplays bound in thick cardboard with her agency's insignia on the front, which might contain a role not so disgusting, not so degrading, not so one-dimensional, not so much the gross misconceptions of another board room full of adolescent boys with their cocks out, stroking them, that she might consider debasing herself with the activity of creating an audition tape, an activity that she, an actress of great skill and increasing prominence, must degrade herself with once or twice a week so she may continue working in an impossible profession making inflated sums of money that allow her to have a drink in the early afternoon, afford many expensive books, and the time to read them. A lifestyle she is accustomed to and one that fills her with a strange sense of dread forever in orbit around the weighty mass of her comfort. Sillyboi stands at the front door and his legs seize with painful cramps.

Ms. Slow Death opens the door and looks surprised.

"Oh. Hello," she says.

"Hi. What?" Already he can tell this is not the right tone.

"What do you mean 'what?' Weirdo. I said, hello."

"Sorry."

"This is off to a strange start."

"It's not. You just looked surprised to see me."

"I'm not surprised." Ms. Slow Death hates being told how she looks or is feeling.

"Okay."

Something resembling warmth spreads across her face.

"Hi Silly."

"Hi. It's been two years."

Sillyboi remembers their last interaction a year after they broke up. Sillyboi was under the impression that all—or at least most—was repaired between them, until one evening she biked to his apartment and sat down sweaty on his couch to tell him something few people have had the courage to tell him: she was still mad, furious, none of her rage had subsided, their relationship had taxed her, he cheated, lied, and worst of all, let his rage get the best of him. When he should have celebrated her successes, he could only lament his failures. When they should have uncorked bottles of champagne in honor of the money she would soon be making, he himself was becoming uncorked and spraying his rage—if only it was semen he sprayed, but no, his emasculation was total—all over the walls of her Silver Lake apartment, which she paid for and he moped within, lamenting the most common problem that can arise between two actors; that she was momentarily more successful than he; that she was getting the opportunities and he was being passed over; that on the red carpet they were calling her name and not his; that directors were requesting her, not him, and that in the most fickle of all professions, fortune was shining on her: beautiful and gifted, smart and unselfconscious.

"It was scary, Silly!" Ms. Slow Death said. "You were completely out of control, there was that time, near the end, you were screaming at me, and our eyes both landed on a knife, a sharp knife, on the coffee table."

"What knife? I don't remember a knife!"

"Don't play dumb, you saw it, we both saw it, it was a very impactful moment for me! You saw the knife and I swear you were this close, this fucking close!"

"This close to what? To cutting you a piece of salami maybe!"

"Oh, don't joke. This is no joke, you were about to, I can't even say it, it's too awful."

"You think I'm insane? You're describing someone psychotic!"

"I thought you were going to attack me! Do you have any idea, any idea how horrible that feels, how frightening that is? To think your boyfriend, the person you love, is this close to stabbing you!?"

Am I here for another beating? Sillyboi wonders. *I'm a new man. Should I show you my tattoo? I've remade myself. I've made progress. I spell my name differently!*

"No, it hasn't." Ms. Slow Death corrects him.

"What?"

"It hasn't been two years."

"I think it has."

"Jesus."

"Yeah."

Ms. Slow stifles a laugh.

"What?"

"Nothing."

"Do I look strange or something?" *Do I look different*, is what he wants to ask.

"No. You look exactly the same. I look different. Come in. I'd rather not stand in the doorway. There are a couple of people on this block I'm trying to avoid."

Sillyboi follows Ms. Slow Death into the apartment and sits on a stool across from a sofa where she roosts, script pages and tissues radiating in concentric circles from an indentation the shape of her ass. On a glass coffee table with Lucite legs, is a bottle of sancerre and a short glass on a cork coaster.

"I would offer you a drink but I know you don't want one." Ms. Slow Death scolds.

"Thanks anyway."

"You still smoke weed all the time? I actually have some."

"You bought weed?"

"No, someone left it here." Sillyboi wonders who it was and if abandoning weed was a romantic gesture.

"I'm taking a break from smoking."

"Really?"

"Yeah."

Ms. Slow Death glares at him, unconvinced. Sillyboi wants to mention how much he would like to smoke but, remembering his tattoo, feels a surge of confidence. Sillyboi molds his face into the expression of a masculine winner. She laughs, so pure and unselfconscious he remembers why many have raised millions, hired crew, and recorded her laugh in high definition to preserve it for future generations and assure them that, even in 2015, there were those who laughed without irony.

"What is that face you're making?" she asks through laughter.

"What face?"

"You're so weird."

"That's a compliment. It's cool to be weird."

"You look constipated."

"Fuck you."

"Fuck you."

"Sorry."

If only Sillyboi could be mean. But no, he can only be beautiful, which is often misinterpreted as mean. Sillyboi wonders what he is doing at Ms. Slow Death's apartment, failing at his new improved (tattooed) personality. As if the climax of their worst argument hadn't had them both glancing at a knife near salami and soft gorgonzola on the coffee table, hungry for battle. As if he wasn't humiliated by how he frightened her. As if they hadn't been in love, moved in, and went to sleep angry and horny as their affection soured to acrimony at the embarrassing detail of Sillyboi's chronically flaccid penis. The erection that refused to manifest under Ms. Slow Death's charisma. Then, without warning, an element of tenderness enters the room.

Ms. Slow Death pulls her legs to her chest, and smiles. Sillyboi smiles back. Ms. Slow Death blinks. Sillyboi blinks back. And whatever once connected them is reestablished. Maybe there is a reason he's there. The criminal revisits the scene of the crime. Sometimes, the prosecutor pays respect. Her mouth opens, she has something to say, but the impulse is muted.

"I need your help with something," she says.

"With what?"

"An audition tape."

"Really?"

"Yeah."

"That's why you wanted to talk to me?

She narrows her eyes.

"No. That's not why."

"It's not?"

"No."

"Okay."

"What I had to say, I don't want to say anymore." Ms. Slow Death laughs. "But I do need help with this self-tape."

A true actor is a rare thing. She can neither act nor pretend. She is like a bathtub that only produces water at the perfect temperature, neither a degree too hot or cold, it feels like nothing on the skin. Sillyboi balances a small stack of script pages on his lap, and shoots on his phone as Ms. Slow Death sits on a stool in front of a blank wall as water—ideal in every way—accumulates around their feet, saturating the wall-to-wall carpeting. *I am going to smoke weed tonight,* Sillyboi decides. *Fuck this whole sobriety thing, it has not done any good. My life is the same consistent hum of bad things happening.*

(Hold on. One second. My mother is calling me. My mother is reading what I write as I write it; and may, from time to time, interject and give her opinion.

"Hello?"

"Hi sweetie."

"Hi mommela, how's it going?"

"Great, but just curious, were you in a bad mood today at Juice Press?"

After working out at the gym in the basement of my parent's apartment building, I decided not to join them for lunch, but to live my own life and drop a handful of gold bullion at the neighborhood smoothie dispensary to flush my system of toxins and prolong life. As I waited for my smoothie to blend, in walked my parents, happy to see me. I was less happy.

"All this stuff about pot, in your book. Is that true?"

"What do you mean, true?"

"It's just a lot. If I didn't know any better, I would think your protagonist has a drug problem. It's a little disturbing. Is this based on life?"

"Do you know that is one of the very worst things you can accuse a writer of? Fiction is fiction. Do not make the mistake of confusing fiction with reality."

"Okay. But couldn't you see where I would have this feeling? Reading a book where you talk about pot on almost every page?"

"Mom, I...this is why I can't have you reading this! Please! I know it's...will you just stop reading? I know you mean well. But can we please make this your first and last intrusion?"

"Okay." She is not satisfied.

"I am indicting a whole generation of stoners. This is an anti-drug book. I don't want to have to spell it out!"

"Okay. I won't bring it up again. I'm not trying to impede your creativity. I'm not. I am just actually curious about this one detail, as a reader."

"It's cultural criticism!"

"I get it now, thank you for clarifying."

"Okay, can we talk more later?"

"I hope you're not angry."

"No, I am really not."

"Are you sure?"

"Completely positive."

"Okay well, I love you so much. I was really enjoying reading."

"I'm so glad."

"I love you baby."

"Love you." I say and hang up.

But don't get me wrong, dear mother, I am an addict, not to pot and its retard fumes, my addiction is to detoxifying smoothies! My addiction is to longevity! I am addicted to life, dear mother, you succeeded in raising a super-healthy life addict!)

THREE

In the airport, after having his body radiated in the name of
national security, TSA-sanctioned waves tempting his young
smoothie-fed cells to mutate into young smoothie-fed cancer
—an x-ray image of his cock added to the database of
passenger's cocks and pussies the TSA is hoarding and
snickering at—Sillyboi puts in his filthy ear buds to play
Future's new album *Dirty Sprite 2*. Sillyboi only listens to
Trap; where masculinity is valued and references to tribal
grievances and lethal quarrels are not always symbolic, he
imagines. The popular music of the American id. Sillyboi
likes to imagine he is Future, beautiful, Black, with long
dreads and feline features, living as pure persona. Too great
for an ordinary name. Future who calls himself Future: all
we hope for, fear, and enumerate soft-voiced in our prayers.
Rock-stars are corny dead white guys, thinks Sillyboi, as the
opening verse to *Blow a Bag* plays in his earphones. Sillyboi
feels compelled to consider what tragedies may underwrite
his fantasy relationship with Future. *What does his music
endorse if not nihilism, addiction, and misogyny?* He feels

compelled to think. He doubts his information channels—
Spotify, Rap Genius, Wikipedia—grant him access to the
truth. *Is it wrong to seek refuge from my sterile world of
smoothies? Is it wrong to pray at the altar of a popular poet
and feel momentarily relieved of myself? Is there something
inappropriate about my love for Future?*

In his imagination, Sillyboi is on a couch in a trap
house sitting next to Future who sips from a Styrofoam cup
as light catches the diamond bezel of his Audemars Piguet
wristwatch. On a table is a brick of white wrapped in
cellophane, white like Sillyboi, who has never felt whiter
than he does from within this fantasy.

"Hey, Future," he says.

Future nods. Sillyboi isn't sure how to fantasize about
this. Is he surrounded by kingpins with weapons, about to
witness weight being moved? Or, are the kingpins actors
outfitted to look like big movers? Are the guns toys filled
with caps? Sillyboi waits for a director to appear, or the
house to be stormed by DEA agents.

> *Sold over a million dimes, hangin' in the cut*
> *sold over a million dimes*
> *I don't give a fuck*

Future sings. Sillyboi enters the plane, finds his seat
and settles down next to a blonde woman in work-out
clothing, texting. The sun coming through the window next
to her is so bright she must use her hand as a visor to shield
her face from the glare. Sillyboi glances at her screen hoping
to catch a glimpse of something too personal for public

consumption but can only read one mundane text:

Don't be. It wasn't like that at all.

Is anything as it presents itself, Sillyboi wonders as he closes his eyes and leans his head on the stiff airline seat equal parts bored and enthralled by life's endless stream of mysteries. Sillyboi gives Future a warm embrace. He wants to leave the trap house before the DEA arrives or the director calls action.

"I'm really glad we met. I love *Dirty Sprite 2*. It's my favorite album ever," Sillyboi says, weeping tears of joy.

"Thanks," Future says, a little uncomfortable.

"Oh, and I don't mind that maybe you've broken the law in your life. I'm sure you only broke laws I didn't agree with. And, in a way, I feel like you did it for me. So I wouldn't have to."

Future nods, eager for the conversation to be over.

Sillyboi is asleep before the plane takes off.

•

The plane lands and Sillyboi sends two texts: the first is to mommy and daddy, the second to Chloe, and both contain the message that he is alive and well and back in the city.

Can't wait to see you, silly! Chloe texts.

Can't wait to see it! she adds followed by a long string of yellow face with heart eyes emojis punctuated by Munch's *The Scream* emoji. Sillyboi hopes the line for taxis isn't too long.

The line for taxis is too long.

Should Sillyboi care what his parents think about his new tattoo? Who expects their parents to approve? Sillyboi's thoughts are humiliating—mommy, daddy, mommy, daddy —an incessant stream of infantile screaming. *I am castrated! I crave! I crave! I crave!* Is this tattoo yet another failed attempt to cut the umbilical cord? Disgusted with himself, Sillyboi takes out his cracked iPhone to try more of the same antidote. Future's voice blots his anxiety.

Dirty Soda, Spike Lee, white girl, Ice-T...

A perfect quintet of drug references, satisfying and elegant, put his guilt on pause. Sillyboi climbs into a taxi. He closes his eyes. Back in the trap house, Future is speaking to Sillyboi in the calm tone of a spiritual guru.

"Poor misguided Sillyboi. The evidence of your autonomy is permanently etched on your stomach. Could there be a more potent reminder of your personhood?"

"Please Future," Sillyboi says, "replace my self-eviscerating Jewish American megalomania with the self-inflating megalomania of the Black American trap artist! You, Future are Beyonce for men!"

The hairs on the back of Sillyboi's neck rise to attention as the first verse drops:

> *I just fucked your bitch in some Gucci flip flops*
> *I just had some bitches and I made 'em lip-lock*
> *I just took a piss and I seen codeine coming out*

We got purple Actavis, I thought it was a drought.

The drought Future refers to is the lack of promethazine-laced codeine produced by the pharmaceutical manufacturer Actavis who recently pulled their signature brand of cough syrup from distribution after trap artists like Future started to represent their brand in a way that made the company uncomfortable: normalizing its recreational overuse. Very off-brand. But there are positive consequences; free advertising, of course! In a surprising reversal, Actavis hires Future as a spokesperson. Future steps into the bright white void of a television commercial.

"Hello America. Future here. Yeah, it's true. When I take a piss, I see codeine coming out. And that codeine was made by my **[REDACTED]** over at Actavis. These chemist **[REDACTED]** make all sorts of drugs you should use but only when you're actually sick." Future laughs and sips from the white Styrofoam cup he holds out of frame. "Buy that good **[REDACTED]** at your local pharmacy and, when you do, tell 'em Future sent you." A graphic pops on screen: "Actavis" in gold letters crusted with purple diamonds as a gravel-throated announcer, white as a picket fence—the ideal father, the protector of fragile ambitions, the glue that holds your organs in place, the silky baritone to stitch up your wounds—chimes in, speaking with supernatural pace over Future's smiling face.

"Sip drugs, have fun, get rich: Actavis! Tell them Future sent you, you coddled baby with only one tattoo."

Sillyboi's phone vibrates with a call from Chloe. He answers after the second ring.

"Hi baby."

"Baby!"

"Hi, sweet baby."

"How was the flight my sweet man?"

"Pretty nice! I slept the whole way through."

"I bet that was cute. How was the shoot?" Chloe asks. (Sillyboi was not only in LA to get his name tattooed. Sillyboi was there to play a tiny role in a big movie that I would go into great detail describing were it not for the non-disclosure agreement Sillyboi signed affirming he would conceal even the most insignificant detail about the production before its release. Sillyboi was hired to act in Movie X as he bears a striking resemblance to the star and, in one hideously brief flashback, portrays the star as a college student who, carrying school books across the quad, witnesses an injustice.) Sillyboi can imagine the concavity of Chloe's dimples but the rest of her is blank.

"It was fine." He says.

"Just fine?"

"All I did was grimace really."

"Oh baby. I bet it was a great grimace."

"It was pretty good."

Sillyboi tries to remember Chloe. Faces emerge in his consciousness: Celeste, lips puckered; Ms. Slow Death, mouth bent in consternation; his mother calling him, worried.

And, then she appears: Chloe, clear skin, round forehead, Asian eyes, and small bubble of a nose over the lips, an upward slope and counterpoint to Sillyboi's sharp Semitic beak.

Sillyboi steps out of the cab, grinding his teeth, and concludes his grimace on the Hollywood set will be his final fake action. Never again will he submit himself to the bipolarity of the acting profession. Never again will he humiliate himself at the feet of another jaded casting director and spill his soul to an industry that sees him as scrap to be bought and sold at the auction of human souls. There is enough money in his bank account to afford him time to find another way to capitalize on his imagination.

Like all millennials, Sillyboi believes himself to be in possession of the highest quality imagination. *What worlds exist inside me,* Sillyboi muses, *I am in awe of my capacity to create and it gives me so much joy and also so much angst!* Sillyboi longs for the day when his genius is no longer undercover and he can walk down the street in New York, Berlin, Tokyo, or Dubai and feel the energy of hundreds, thousands, or hundreds of thousands of probing eyeballs. But what excites Sillyboi even more than fame is the future contents of his future thoughts. The coherent tapestry of his future genius. *Oh, the riches I will unleash unto the world will leave no one unmoved, either admiration or disgust, I will provoke strong feelings. My work will flood academia! On the summit of a manicured hill somewhere posh, an institute will be erected in my name. The Sillyboi Institute for Genius. And after the complete works of my unedited thoughts are published and released, the world will have a brand new philosophy, a redefinition of every foundational idea, a towering achievement kept safe for posterity in The Sillyboi Institute for Genius. Or The Institute for Silly Thinkers. Or The Institute for Sillyboi The Genius &*

His Silly Acolytes. Or The Sillian School for The Preservation of Silly Thought. Or whichever name I choose once my philosophy is codified. In fact, language may soon be extinct, replaced by pictographs related to thoughts and actions associated with moral excellence.

Sillyboi will be the architect of these new morally excellent pictographs, of course, and the architect of the Institute and surrounding campus. But first, he must decide whether to study architecture or hire the best architecture firm and give them a bunch of really great ideas.

Almost as soon as Sillyboi opens the door, Chloe throws her arms around his neck and peppers his face with a warm spray of kisses.

"Do you like it?" Sillyboi lifts his shirt to present his new tattoo.

Chloe is silent.

"Oh my god," she says and bursts into a fountain of laughter and tears.

The second thing Chloe and Sillyboi must do is have sex. They are young and healthy and what should people with healthy bodies, not yet impacted by disease, do but seek constant pleasure? Sillyboi and Chloe lie in bed, their faces pink with dollar-store Christmas lights. Chloe inspects his new stomach.

"This is so good," she says, "so clean. I can't believe you actually got this."

"I know."

"Do you feel different? Like, more yourself? More badass?

"Yeah." He nods. "Definitely more myself. Definitely

more badass."

"Oh, Silly." Chloe lays her head on his chest smiling.

"More myself. More badass." Sillyboi repeats for emphasis and quickly falls asleep.

FOUR

Chloe cannot fall asleep. A throb of images flicker: Sillyboi texting Celeste, looking at her Instagram, making her cum with his mouth, arousing in her the suspicion that the man sleeping next to her cannot be trusted. *What was Sillyboi actually doing in L.A?* Chloe wonders. Resting near the foot of their bed is Sillyboi's phone and in it, Chloe believes she could find the answers to her questions. But the mechanism that compels some toward confrontation— making them well suited to leadership positions or Twitter— is either broken or absent in Chloe, and she almost prefers the anxious activity of speculation to the fatal calm of true knowledge.

Chloe remembers an evening, a week ago, when Sillyboi appeared at Super Happy Tattoo to pick her up after another day of menial labor as the shop's apprentice.

Chloe reclined on a large mechanized chair, buried in her phone and burning with jealousy to see the work of superior tattooers splashed across her feed. Looking up, she saw Sillyboi in an identical sweatshirt to hers: oversized

Champion zip-up hoodie, black.

"Silly!" she shouted, and wrapped her arms around his neck.

"Hi baby," he says, gripping her midsection.

"Hi baby."

"Hi baby."

"Hi baby."

The conversation could have gone on like this, two words over and over, forever, until Chloe broke the repetition with a laugh of what at first felt like genuine happiness, until an unexpected quiver of dread pulsed in the bottom of her esophagus. It was a feeling so faint that to be banished to nonexistence required little more than a subtle repositioning of the face.

Chloe and Sillyboi walked home down Wilson Avenue past new condominiums with steel and glass facades. Everywhere they looked people were posting photos to social media. Chloe and Sillyboy pressed into each other proclaiming their devotion. And the friction produced by the spot where their faces rubbed together burned away the anxiety of their attachment. She held his body against her own and the thought *this is the feeling that makes death okay* looped in her psyche.

Chloe and Sillyboi passed even more phones; now appraising photos, matching their value against other photos, inadequate when set against the worst photo on the most envied profile; but superior, thank God, when set against any photo on the trash heap of irrelevant profiles Chloe and Sillyboi both despise.

And, as her fingers dented his shoulder; as their boots

struck the pavement in unison; as the smoothness of her cheek chafed against his stubble; in this moment of closeness, Chloe knew Sillyboi was preoccupied with himself. Chloe imagined an application paired with an implant that could live inside Sillyboi's brain and transmit his thoughts to a podcast. People all over the world would subscribe to this service with its algorithm that parses a partner's thoughts and compiles those tabbed as relevant; thoughts relating to betrayal, to unspeakable desires, and to unshared criticisms about the other's genitals.

"What are you thinking?" she finally asked.

"Nothing."

"That's not true."

"I'm thinking I love you."

"That's not true."

"Of course it is."

"I know you love me. But that's not what you were thinking just now."

"It was."

"Why don't you ever ask me about my day?"

Sillyboi cocked his head and molded his features into what he hoped was an expression of astonishment, completely benign, and without any of the subtle tensions of reproach.

"Doesn't it just, like, go without saying I want to hear how your day went?"

"It doesn't go without saying, no."

"I love you, of course I'm curious about your day. Why do I have to offer up a formal request? My family constantly shares bits and pieces of information, that's how it is with intimate relationships."

"I wish your fucking family wasn't your only model for intimate relationships."

Chloe took out her phone and opened Instagram. The last photo she posted was a selfie—taken at work—lips pursed, eyes bored, with the caption "hey fam, quick update, we all might be possessed!" The photo received one-hundred-and-forty-nine likes in three hours. Chloe was pleased with that number and scrolled through the list of appreciative accounts for those that might be important: tattooers, artists, socialites, or, heaven-willing, corporate entities, any account with a followership greater than her own, and whose attention might raise her status. There were a few such accounts scattered among the untouchables. *I have more followers than most (3,456) but far less followers than I will have in a year*, Chloe thought. *In a year, my art will be so great and I will be so hot, my profile will boast the life-affirming "K"* (10.5K is the number she's manifesting), *the "K" that makes you cool. I will be seen. I will be desired. I will be liked and commented on.* Chloe liked to tell herself Instagram is not important and frequently shit talked friends whose lives revolved around their social media value, but she craved that value. She craved the life-affirming "K." She needed to look back on her life and know she won the primary race of her time. *I am not shallow,* Chloe thought. *For me, this is business. My tattoos will make my Instagram famous and when they are each a work of art, my schedule will overflow with appointments, and I will be rich.*

She would make her mark on countless strangers and, in sixty-years-time, all those bodies—once so young and hip, on the brink of extinction, laced with her ink, faded by time, quaint relics of a past aesthetic—will die and her artwork will vanish. But her Instagram will live for eternity as an archive of her life; of the person she was; of the art she made; of her beautiful body; of her beautiful face; of the memes she reposted; proof of her content, status, and existence in time—valuable to tens of thousands of eyeballs.

Chloe got three new followers and was pleased.

"Please tell me about your day?" Sillyboi begged.

"I don't want to. It was boring."

"Something must have happened."

"My friend was coming in to get a tattoo. I was really nervous about it."

"How was it?"

"She didn't show up."

"That sucks."

"It's okay."

"What was it?"

"Some flash I did. A lady head. With roses. She wanted it full color.

"That sounds cool."

"It's stupid."

"I'm sure it's not stupid."

"I'm not confident with color."

"Do you think she'll reschedule?"

"Probably not. People who don't show up for tattoos fucking suck. And no one came in to work till, like, four o' clock, so I was alone in the shop watching WorldStarHipHop Vine compilations for literally hours."

"Sounds fun."

"Do you watch WorldStar ever?"

"Sometimes. For the music videos."

"You should watch it for the Vines. It's like, these kids getting into horrible fights, anywhere you can think of, in classrooms, on rooftops, in the mall, on train tracks with trains rushing towards them, like, really vicious fights. And, behind them kids are chanting 'do it for the vine, do it for the vine!' You got to watch if you want to stay current. Could be a good movie idea somewhere in there."

"Could be."

"Otis came in at four-thirty. He wakes up at, like, three p.m."

"Jesus."

"Yeah. We had a pretty interesting discussion. But I feel sort of strange about it now."

"What was the subject?"

"I don't know if I can go into it."

"Please."

Chloe inhaled to speak, then deflated.

"Tell me," Sillyboi pleaded.

"Well, basically, we were talking about how once you have a lot of tattoos you become an object for people. Like, that morning Otis was taking the train back from the supermarket because he had to carry a whole bunch of paper towels and garbage bags and just, like, shit we needed for the shop and this woman came up to him, literally as he was holding all of these shopping bags full of shit, she was, like, in her late-thirties, white, possibly from Long Island, seemed sober, but she started to, like, ask him if she could touch his arm."

"Wow."

"That's fucked up. And, Otis was, like, no, you can't touch me. Of course not. You can't just go up to a stranger on the train and ask to touch them. It's like if you went up to a Black person and asked to touch their hair or, like, I don't know if you wanted to take a photo of an Asian's eyes."

"Is that similar though?"

"Yes! Just because I made the decision to have tattoos doesn't turn me into something a stranger can touch. And, the fucking white woman took out her cell phone and snapped a picture of him. So fucked."

"I don't know."

"Trust me, it's fucked, you can't touch people or take photos of them because you're fascinated by the way they look."

"My mom takes photos of any baby in the wild she thinks is cute."

"That's weird."

"My mother's old. It's benign."

"Sure."

"But, like, do you not see anything in the decision to get covered from the neck down in tattoos, as Otis has, as, like, some sort of desire to be looked at? Or, at least noticed?"

"Getting a tattoo has nothing to do with being noticed."

"Well, maybe not, but isn't it sort of some form of exhibitionism? Like do you have tattoos all over your arms and neck so people won't look at them?"

"What?"

"How can you exist in the world, covered in tattoos,

and expect people not to look at them?"

"You don't get it."

"Okay. Maybe I don't."

"It's not exhibitionism."

"Okay. What is it?"

"I need to get out of the city! I miss nature! I can't stand living here sometimes in this city. I need fresh air! Can we please rent a car soon and take a trip? Even for a day? Anywhere."

"Sure."

"You don't want to."

"I do."

"You don't."

"Everyone sort of wants to be looked at."

"I don't."

"Otis certainly wants to be looked at."

"He doesn't want to be touched on the train by some bridge-and-tunnel bitch."

There was a game Sillyboi and Chloe played on the flight of stairs to their apartment. The game involved Chloe trying to shove her fingers through the denim of Sillyboi's pants and into his asshole. It wasn't so much a game as it was a reoccurring piece of private theater in which the couple plays and replays a core theme of their relationship. On display in this game was Chloe's desire to inhabit Sillyboi's darkest most intimate interior. Sillyboi bounded up the stairs, protesting through his laughter. Sillyboi swatted away her invading hand and clenched his anus. He squealed, screamed, and disturbed all the neighbors in the building.

Later, in bed, Chloe lectured Sillyboi about how to execute permanent marks, flawlessly, on a surface as idiosyncratic as the body. "A line must be executed in one pass. That's how Rubendall makes a line—any of the greats, really—in one pass, without a pause. Check out his lines." Chloe lifts her arm to reveal a rose framed with leaves on her tricep—this is exhibit A, lecture one, Line Work in Tattooing 101— "once you set out to make a line you should not have to lift the machine until the line is complete. It's nearly impossible. But look at this. That's how this was made. It doesn't look human. It looks like a stamp."

"You'll be as good as Rubendall soon."

"No!" Chloe exploded with aggression, directed as much to herself as to Sillyboi, sprung from the pure well of anger that is ambition. "You don't understand how hard that is! How many fucking years it takes!"

"Sorry. I don't get it then."

"It's, like," Chloe dragged the joint and wrapped her legs around him, "when you tattoo you have to become the machine. Your arm, your whole body, it's got to be, like, an extension of the machine. It cannot be separate. When you think of the machine as something apart from yourself that's when you fuck up. You got to allow the vibrations into your body. Like, for the past few months I've been fighting with it, I think. Trying to turn the machine into a pen, and I didn't realize I was doing it at the time, but I was fighting the reality of the tool. It's hard to understand unless you've tried it. Felt yourself fight the vibrations and then allow the vibrations. With no separation. You and the machine, both vibrating. But I think I might be getting it, finally. Or, like, starting to get it, at least."

Sillyboi brushed hair away from her almond shaped eyes and moved his finger over her lips. Sillyboi took her in, enthralled by her otherness, overcome with desire and envy. Chloe is covered in tattoos: her fingers, her forearms, her neck. She is one with her art. Sillyboi wished he could be like Chloe and cover himself with tattoos, her skin, abolish the distance between them, and merge completely.

"I have to stop talking so much to clients. It's not proper. And, I think it's contributing to my anxiety, like, when I get tattooed by Ryan, who is fucking amazing, he becomes, like, a different person. He isn't my friend or even a person. He's the machine. He won't even say my name. He calls me kid. 'Hey kid. You ready, kid?' No joke. I'm nobody. I'm meat and he's the machine. It's hot."

"It is?"

"Ryan's married! His wife is pregnant. It's hot in, like, I fucking admire it so much way."

"You'd still hit it."

"No, I wouldn't."

"If you were single?"

"He's married!"

"If he was single."

Chloe allowed herself a vulgar thought.

"Oh, come on!"

"Sure, if he was single and I was single. He could get it."

"Now I'm jealous."

Chloe turns to face him.

"Good. I like it when you're jealous."

"Yeah?"

"It makes me super horny."

"Why?"

"Because now we're even. I'm always jealous. I'm jealous when you walk down the street and I'm not there. I'm jealous of every girl who looks at you."

After sex, Chloe waddled to the bathroom. Sillyboi followed her down their long apartment to the shower, almost too small to accommodate them both. Chloe put her face in the stream to rub away her eye makeup. Mascara ran down her cheeks.

"Am I a raccoon?"

"A fuckable raccoon."

Chloe feels a surge of warmth for Silly. But how can she ignore the holes: one above the toilet and the other in the door opposite the toilet, punched by Sillyboi who cannot remember the subject of the outburst that made them. The holes are dark portals. Prying eyes spying on the couple as they diddle parts and wipe butts. Wounds through which the lifeblood of the relationship slowly leaks.

Chloe grabs his cock. Water pounds the basin. The lover's mouths meet and the first notes of Justin Bieber's "What Do You Mean?" crash through the silence, through the holes, and into the shower, disrupting the lovers.

Their neighbor is a forty-year-old Dominican named Nicole whose temperament exists on a scale that slides between low-grade agitation and unbridled rage and who loves the music of Justin Bieber. Nicole's nighttime habit is to crank her music to rocket launch decibels, wreaking havoc on the building's light sleepers.

•

Now, it is 3:30 a.m. and Chloe is still in bed, unable to sleep. Sillyboi, inches from her, is sound asleep. That he allows himself sleep while she cannot is an act that feels as aggressive as punching holes into drywall. Chloe takes a photo of him, asleep with mouth comically open, opens Instagram, and contemplates posting. She wants to get even; to humiliate him the way she feels humiliated by her preoccupation with him. She closes Instagram. She will not post. She might post later, but not now. Chloe tosses the phone to the bottom of the bed hoping it will strike and wake him to begin the honest discussion she craves.

Nicole's bedroom shares a wall with Chloe and Sillyboi's and, for the past hour, Chloe has endured the piercing melody of Nicole's voice, another element in the symphony, already baroque, in her psyche. Chloe's noise-canceling headphones are dead and she can hear every word Nicole says on the phone, becoming more and more heated. Nicole laughs, her cackle bending like a siren zipping past, accented by heavy footsteps as she walks from her bedroom to another part of her apartment. To re-fill her cup, Chloe imagines, or expel bile.

Chloe crawls to the foot of the bed to retrieve her phone and check the time. 3:33 a.m. Chloe returns to Instagram. Earlier in the evening, against her better judgment, and in conflict with the professional persona she is striving to project, Chloe posted a photo of herself in bed, biting the edge of her t-shirt and pulling it up to reveal a lacy bra underneath. Chloe took the photo two weeks ago but waited until tonight to post. The photo was taken to send to Sillyboi. *I need to stop being a needy girlfriend,* Chloe thinks, disgusted with herself, *this is not who I am. I took this photo so...what? So, he would think of me? So, he would text me? I don't need him to think about me. I need to focus on myself, on my work, and stop being so preoccupied with him.* But still, the thought nags her. *I don't know what he does all day long. Is he really just sitting there, in that coffee shop, writing screenplays? If he is really there, all day long, like he says he is, I know he must be talking to girls. He is a flirt. He thinks I don't see it. I do. Does he think I'm an idiot or is he just that naïve?*

•

When Chloe was a freshman in art school, when she herself was naïve, before she realized the small fortune her parents forfeited to send her to The Steinhardt School at NYU, where the majority of her peers sincerely believed the contents of the Photo Booth on their MacBook Pros was art worthy of considerable praise, Chloe decided her classmates were each like an arm on a monster fed by a mixture of limitless credit and Adderall. Chloe imagined herself at war with the monster and the detailed drawings she brought in for critique, prototypes for the tattoo flash she would soon be drawing, were her weapons, and so superior to the pseudo-post-net-art her classmates paid-to-have-made (Monster Energy Drink patchwork quilts, 3D-printed dildos with Chase Bank emblazoned on the balls, piñatas in the shape of Rush-brand poppers with real poppers inside) that it baffled her when they garnered the opposite reaction. Her drawings, formal and precise, were dismissed as irrelevant, cute, and worst of all, commercial. Chloe didn't want to be a student. She didn't want to throw money at an institution founded on pretense that was, at best, a narrow entry point to the even greater pretension of the Art World. Chloe doubted NYU was an entry point to that exclusive world. It was around this time of doubt, during her first Thanksgiving break, that Chloe got her first tattoo.

Thanksgiving break. Three days with the power to ruin the whole month of November. Only three months into her college experience, the shackles of youth just beginning to fall from her limbs, being forced back to the household she had waited her entire childhood to escape, was a punishment. There are large portions of her senior year she doesn't remember. She knows she took more Xanax than her prescription dictated, and a sensation of floating accompanied everything. Her personality flattened, she slept in class and in between classes. Yes, Xanax made her tired, but sleep also protected her. It was a nice break from the discomfort of being awake. Chloe remembers her drug dealer boyfriend Brandon; chiseled body, Botticelli lips, and the pounds of weed he kept under his bed. Chloe remembers afternoons she stayed at school late to cheat on Brandon with her thirty-four-year-old English teacher, a guy unfortunately named Chris Columbus, in an affair that began the day she turned seventeen. A memory that visits during insomnia and infuses her with guilt and pride. And, of course, she remembers the Christmas when an unusually hard slap from her strict Chinese father left a nasty bruise on her cheek, so that when the vice principal called Chloe's house to inquire about the origin of the mark, her mother had to explain, with an embarrassed laugh, that Chloe was injured by the wild swing of a badminton racquet during a Sunday tournament; a strange event to take place in winter with a foot of snow on the ground. So, Chloe moved in with her best friend Helen and lived at Helen's family's house for the remainder of the year.

In her own family's home, Chloe was a meteorologist who could forecast when an emotional storm was about to break. The syncopated percussion of footsteps was the pressure drop. The sloppy soft shoe of her mother's flats on the carpeted stairs, combined with the sliding sound her wedding band made going down the banister, confirmed her insobriety, as her mother would only deign to grip that strip of wood when she was truly hammered. From the basement, Chloe could hear the television, a sign her father had distanced himself, cemented in himself, until everyone had sobered up. The familiar sound of television conjured a comforting image of her father bathed in blue and red light, his handsome Mandarin face registering exactly no emotion, as a sudden overwhelming fondness developed in her chest. She had to resist the urge to run down the steps and bury her face in his shoulder, breathing and humming into the fabric of his sweater, like she would as a child before everything came between them. But before Chloe could move a step in any direction, her mother appeared before her, breathing wine-scented breath.

"Hello, sweetheart." Her mother's embrace pinned both arms uncomfortably to her body. Chloe couldn't remember the last time she felt her mother's enormous breasts press against her own. Chloe choked back a wave of nausea, repulsed by her mother's thickness, and tried not to breathe in her smell, the sour odor masked only slightly by floral perfume.

"What's going on? Is everything okay?" Chloe's tone was accusatory but a box of wine in her mother's system made her happily tone deaf.

"Everything's great. So happy you're home."

"Okay. Where's dad?"

"Downstairs."

"Why?"

"Hey, Chlo, let's take a little trip downtown?" Chloe was caught off guard.

"What?"

"I want to take you somewhere. You'll drive us, won't you?"

"Mom, I literally just got home."

"When was the last time we did something together? You'll like this. You have your license on you, yes?"

"Why can't you drive?" Chloe was always curious to hear her mother's invented reasoning.

"Sprained my ankle taking groceries up the porch, still hurts, shouldn't push it."

"It's late. What are you trying to do?"

The activity Chloe's mother had in mind, where her mid-life crisis overlapped with Chloe's rebellion, was to share in an unprecedented moment of mother-daughter bonding with an action potentially strong enough to melt the animosity that had frozen the relationship. Chloe's mother had found a tattoo shop in downtown D.C, open for walk-ins, and there they would get matching tattoos. The tattoo they chose was a lotus flower, placed conveniently out of sight given the proportions of most attire, on the back, between the shoulder blades.

•

Sleepless in bed, Chloe floats her hands a few inches over the parts of her body that remind her most of her mother. She has looked up videos of Reiki and this is essentially what the practice looks like, directing spiritual energy into cells through hands, coaxing genes to reject the contribution of a complicated mother. Chloe thinks of her father's ageless face and lean hairless body. His face and hairlessness she inherited, not his shape. *I am going to be fat like my mother*. Chloe hates New Age nonsense, trendy kale juice bullshit. But in this moment, still awake with the sun soon rising, she prays for anything that might help her pass out, even a healing mist on her eyelids, or green light beamed into her heart chakra. Chloe knows her mother is unwell and something fundamental in her is broken. Chloe cannot even think her name, let alone speak it, write it, type it, or search it in the logs of her phone without a painful pricking dread. *My mother,* Chloe thinks, *is the kind of woman who would participate in genocide if she were commanded to do so*. Women to the right, men to the left. She can see her mother's deadly thumb pointing this way and that, presiding over a mass grave without emotion. *She betrayed my father and our entire family. She is broken. How can Sillyboi possibly sleep through this? First, it was our neighbor, and now my thoughts! These are thoughts you wake up for!* Chloe moves her hands, still charged with improvised Reiki, to cast a spell on him. *Wake up Silly, wake up and love me more. Wake up and need me the way I need you to need me, wake up and hold me in your arms. Don't think of other girls. Don't look at other girls on Instagram. Think only of me. Talk only to me. Every girl will become invisible to you. On their faces, on their asses, you will see my face reflected. And your hands will reach into your pocket to take out your phone and send me a selfie so I know you're behaving. But that won't be your motivation for sending me a selfie. You will send me a selfie because you love me and need me to see the love in your eyes. You want to remind me of the way your face looks full of love. The way I feel compelled to show you mine. And, when you can't send a selfie, you will text and your texts will be poetry. 'I love you,' you will text, 'I miss you,' you will text, 'I live to hold you,' you will text, 'you are everything,' you will text. And it will be simple and perfect.*

Chloe stares at him.

Sillyboi is lying on his side, hands pressed together and propped under his cheek like a porcelain figurine of a sleeping angel. Sillyboi is the most beautiful man she has ever seen in person. Suddenly everything around her, their bedroom like a page ripped from an Ikea catalog, feels so far from solid she must conjure something gruesome, a high-definition clip of an ISIS beheading slowed down and close up on the victim's face, to avoid panic.

Chloe hears Nicole through the wall as she enters her bedroom with a man whose quiet bass makes him impossible to understand.

"I called it. These white people is like roaches. I saw it with my own eyes nine years ago. You know I called it, fucking called that shit! As soon as I seen one of those motherfuckers I knew. Roaches. You see one and you know the rest is gonna follow. White people man. And they little Asian-ass girlfriends. They the worst. The fucking worst kind of person on this planet. I'm telling you they is exactly alike. You know when you find one of those little black bugs in yo' kitchen and you know! You know you is gonna keep seeing them motherfuckers! I wish I had some poison or some shit, we could sprinkle the streets with, and get rid of these fucking crackers man."

The man laughs and says something that sounds like, "you know, when you got a dirty Band-Aid, you can't catch the comet." But that can't be right.

"I'm telling you, the day I saw the first cracker on the block, I said a prayer. I said my motherfucking prayers! But I knew it was over." The man says something that sounds like, "you can't beat cola at perfect sin." But Chloe knows that's not it.

"My tia used to sit outside, right there, on Wilson man, play stereo and checkers with those nasty old bitches and old ass motherfuckers. Don't see that no more. Want me out too, wop landlord want me out, so he can get a shiny new cracker in here to pay double." The man says something like, "needle be hard like white chord lover."

Chloe throws off the covers, tiptoes to the wall, and presses her ear against the plaster. "Fuck these kids man! Fighting all the time, fucking all the time, early in the morning, at night, guy screaming at the top of his lungs like he gone kill someone, and she crying. They kicking shit and then they is fucking real loud, bang, bang, bang, bang. It's fucking gross! Like it's happening in my own damn bedroom! And, they potheads, smoking that skank-shit all day long, making the whole building smell like skunk. I hate it! I hate them so much man! I'd kill these motherfuckers! Bash they door down and stab a motherfucker! They think they is running shit! But they not! I fucking run this shit! You hear that neighbors! I FUCKING RUN THIS SHIT!"

Sillyboi sleeps undisturbed while the amber light of dawn breaks over the townhouses on Wilson Avenue. On a rooftop across the street from where Chloe lies awake, a man opens a pigeon coop and releases his flock. The man's birds lift off in unison and carve a pattern of repetition into the sky. The man's pigeons were born and raised in captivity and have only known the routine of the group. Soaring and falling together, it is the rare pigeon that abandons the flock. Sometimes the man wonders if his pigeons notice their status as individual birds or if they perceive themselves as one enormous pigeon and are capable of complex multi-pigeon thoughts with grand and communal pigeon-dreams.

FIVE

The next night, Chloe decides to finish an episode of *Girls* and it is actually pretty funny. The episode concludes with the character played by Donald Glover accusing the character played by Lena Dunham of being racist. Donald Glover accuses Lena Dunham of hooking up with him to release herself of white guilt, as a publicity stunt to remove herself from the list of White Girls Who Are Only Into White Guys or the related list of White People Who Are Secretly Racist. Sillyboi watches over her shoulder, seething with envy at the famous racist and/or non-racist television actors, and motions for her to pass him the joint.

"Are you going to freak out?" She says.

"No, I'm not going to freak out. I want to smoke."

"I thought you said you weren't going to smoke."

"I want to."

"You sure?"

"Yeah."

"Okay." Chloe takes a drag and glances over at a drawing, in progress, on her desk: a naked woman hog tied in Shibari ropes. Sillyboi also looks at the drawing.

"I like that."

Chloe grunts.

"Well, you'll make it good."

"Maybe."

"Whose it for?"

"Some random."

"That's cool."

"I guess."

"They could have chosen any artist in the city, but they chose you. That's awesome."

"I sort of know him. He's a friend of friends."

"Someone you fucked?"

Chloe looks up from her work.

"No."

"Just making sure."

"You think I've fucked everyone. You think I'm such a slut."

"When we started dating you'd always mention how you'd been with a ton of people. Slut's your word. Not mine. I'd never use that word."

"I never told you that."

"You totally did."

"I think I told you I had a lot of boyfriends."

"Sleeping with someone on and off for, like, a month doesn't make them your boyfriend. Can I have the joint, please?"

"If I give it to you, you have to promise not to feel guilty afterwards."

"I won't."

Chloe rolls her eyes and hands him the joint.

Sillyboi inhales and this is the moment every stoner cherishes: the first hit of the day. The cylindrical filter feels novel in your mouth and you delight in its delicate weight, a tiny scepter—for a low-key king—it enlivens your gestures with a flourish. You exhale and straddle the states, sober and stoned, which is to say you are finally entering "the now," "the present moment." Pure sativa with sweet smoke—a hint of mango—and you are overcome by the desire to talk incessantly and selfishly.

But Chloe needs quiet, so you reach for Instagram. Say, didn't you once post an image to Instagram: a 3D-graphic with a whiff of 2003 about it? Oh yes, it was a screenshot from *Second Life* of a woman standing in the Piazza del Marco wearing yellow hard taco shells as shoes. An important image. Ryder Ripps reposted and gave you credit. A miracle! The repost reverberated for days. It imbued your life with worth. You could finally say you understood the image. You understand when an image has special currency and that knowledge places you in an elite group defined by taste. You remember goatse.cx. The proto-troll, the proto-shit-post, the defunct website hosted a single lo-res image; one with value—it shaped you—of a middle-aged man, bent over, face obscured, who, using both hands—gold wedding band visible—pulls his asshole open to Coke can circumference exposing the inside of his rectum like a sliced pomegranate or the topography of an Airheads Extremes® Rainbow Berry Slurpee. Yes, that is a fine example of an image with intrinsic value. You are constantly in search of the image in lineage with goatse. The image that will transform your Instagram into Art.

"I was trying to make you like me." Chloe says.

Sillyboi lowers his phone.

"What? When?"

"When we met. I probably told you I was a slut because I was trying to make you like me."

"Why would that make me like you?"

"I don't know." Chloe continues to draw. "I was nervous you wouldn't like me so I said a lot of stupid shit." Chloe pushes her drawing to the side.

Sillyboi crawls to where she is sitting and pushes his face between her legs. Chloe closes her thighs around his head, squeals, and ejects his mouth from the vicinity of her cunt.

"I'm on my period."

"So?"

"Can we fuck in the shower?"

"Can't we fuck on the bed?"

"My period."

"I don't care."

"I do."

Chloe returns to drawing while Sillyboi retreats to the bathroom where he may be committing another betrayal. Banish the thought and become the machine, Chloe. She takes out tracing paper, translucent, and lays it over another piece of tracing paper that contains the first draft of her design. She places both pieces of paper over a light board, turns on the light, and illuminates the lines to draw a second draft. Will she trust herself when her machine is breaking flesh, no forgiving paper to absorb her mistakes?

Chloe observes her revision and is filled with doubt. She picks up the joint and walks to the bathroom. The toilet flushes and Sillyboi swings the bathroom door open with divine innocence on his face. Chloe sees his phone in his hand. He would be naked were he not holding his phone and a bottle of moisturizer.

"Don't put too much on."

"Of course not."

Sillyboi rubs a layer of lotion on his healing tattoo.

"What were you doing in there?"

"What?"

How can she trust any expression from a face so practiced in deception? Sillyboi continues to rub lotion on his stomach gazing at his reflection in the mirror: sucking in his cheeks, narrowing his eyes, jutting out his jaw, and making a more rigid and masculine mask of his face.

"Stop making that face!"

"What face?"

"What were you doing in the bathroom with your phone? Were you on Instagram?"

"Would that be a problem if I was? You're always on Instagram."

"I am not always on Instagram. You're on Instagram way more than I am on Instagram."

"That is patently false. You post, like, five pictures a day and you flaunt your tits and shit. I have what, like, five followers? And I never post anything."

"But you lurk! You're always lurking! You're a lurker!"

"I am not a lurker!"

Chloe's stomach contracts with the need to express a torrent of sobs.

"Were you looking at girls?"

"Jesus, no! I was reading the news."

"Were you texting Celeste?"

"Have you lost your mind? Do you seriously think I was in the bathroom, texting another girl, in our house, with you right outside just after I was talking about how badly I wanted to fuck?! Do you think I am the sickest, most deranged person who ever lived?!"

"Show me your phone."

"What?"

"You heard me. Show me your phone. If you weren't looking at girls, then show me."

"No."

"If you weren't doing anything wrong, you should have no problem showing me."

"Would I ever ask to see your phone?"

"This isn't about my phone, it's about your phone."

"Show me your phone then."

"You could see my phone any time. You could look through it all you want. I have nothing to hide."

"Really Chloe? I could look through every single one of your texts and find nothing objectionable?"

"You wouldn't!"

"Guys are constantly texting you!!"

"I never text guys!"

"You probably delete them!"

"Stop trying to take the focus off yourself!"

"I'm not!"

"I want to see your phone."

"I am not going to do that."

"Then you're lying to me."

"Do you have any concept of how incredibly immature this is? To force me to show you my phone? Just on principle, I won't do it."

"Do you realize how incredibly immature it is to be jerking off to girls on Instagram while you live with your girlfriend!

"Fine! Here! Take the thing! Do whatever you want with it! I honestly don't care!" Sillyboi thrusts his phone into Chloe's hands. In the second before his decision to give up his phone—and with it the sanctity of his digital privacy— Sillyboi must have imagined he had, in fact, scrubbed his history and that his search bar would not bear the residue of incriminating searches. Or, perhaps he wanted Chloe to see the traces of his transgressions, to begin the process of unraveling or healing or whatever would take place once the dirt was out from under the Gram.

Chloe grips his phone. She taps the screen.

"Oh my god! I knew it." Chloe's face twists to a furious smile. Sillyboi rips his phone from her hands, scratching her index finger on its sharp broken edge. If only this event took place six months in the future, Sillyboi's phone upgraded to the iPhone 6, with rounded edges less prone to fracture, then Chloe's finger would have been spared. Chloe collapses onto the couch, holding her finger, and staring at it, horrified.

"Fuck! What the fuck? You didn't have to grab it!"

Sillyboi cannot speak.

"This isn't good! You sprained it! You asshole! I have to tattoo tomorrow! Now I have to cancel!"

"You can't cancel!"

"I can't tattoo like this! My finger is fully fucked because of you!"

"Let me see. I'm sure it's okay."

Chloe leaps off the couch, rushes into her office, and slams the door. Nicole turns on Justin Bieber—every night like church bells—and the apartment quakes with "Sorry."

Sillyboi feels a burst of pleasant energy. *I could walk out, right now, and leave her,* Sillyboi thinks. But instead he walks to Chloe's office to absolve. He pushes the door open. Chloe is hunched over her desk, noise-canceling headphones on, air redolent of marijuana, drawing.

"Chloe?" Sillyboi taps her on the shoulder. She slides off the headphones and lifts her gaze, flat and bloodshot, to meet his.

"I'm sorry." He says.

"I canceled my appointment."

"Why did you do that?"

"My finger. It's fucked."

"But you need the money."

"Yeah."

"And the practice."

"Yeah."

"So, you can't cancel. Your finger is fine. It will be better in the morning."

Chloe speaks softly.

"You don't get it. I can't tattoo with a fucked-up finger. It's permanent. Do you get that? If I fuck up, that's a permanent mistake."

"I know. But you're drawing now so it must not be that bad."

The sound of a car blasting Future's *Colossal* drives slowly down Wilson Avenue.

I had to go to work with heavy metal
I done seen dead bodies in the ghetto

"Why are you looking at girls on Instagram?"

"I'm not."

"Silly. I saw. You are. You're looking at so many girls. Girls you fucked. You're looking at Celeste."

"I don't even remember looking at them. Would I let you look at my phone if I was actually doing something I shouldn't be doing? Like, lusting after girls online?"

"But that's what you were doing."

"Baby, just because I searched, at one time, some girls I used to know, doesn't mean I was lusting."

"Why were you looking at Celeste?"

"She's my friend."

"Your friend you want to fuck."

"That's not true. She's a colleague. I have to keep in touch with people I've worked with."

"A colleague you want to fuck."

"She's a filmmaker also. It's a good contact. Honestly, you can't tell me who I can and can't be friends with, especially people who could potentially be important for my career."

"Are you going to do another film with her?"

"I don't know. Maybe. Probably not."

"Not if you're with me you won't."

"Chloe please, who knows what's gonna happen, it's not a big deal I looked at her Instagram once."

"What about the others? I saw others. That fucking Tumblr princess with the green hair? I know you fucked her."

"Are you seriously trying to tell me you don't look at guys you've slept with? That's not something you've ever done?"

"I don't."

"That's not true. You're lying to me right now." Chloe takes her phone and offers it to Sillyboi.

"Look at my phone."

"No."

"You think I look at guys, then go ahead, look at my phone. I have nothing to hide. Take it."

"I don't need to."

"Take my phone."

"No Chloe."

"Look through my texts, look through my history, look at my Instagram."

"I know I would find something."

"You wouldn't!"

"Okay!"

"You won't find a thing!"

Later that night, after tacking another handwritten apology to the place above her desk accumulating an ample collection of handwritten apologies—a barely-legible quilt of guilt—Chloe relents and places a dirty towel on the bed so she can please him, menstrual blood be damned. Sillyboi forces his cock so far down her throat she nearly vomits. Chloe gets on top and, with her hands around his neck, cuts off his air, grinding into him with violent erratic movements that nearly sprain his cock. After sex, she goes to wash off the blood while he, stoned and exhausted, opts to sleep bloody and redolent of his woman. Chloe returns from the shower scented marzipan by Dr. Bonner. Sillyboi is almost asleep.

"Silly?"

Sillyboi grunts.

"Can I ask you a question?"

"Of course."

"Do you still like my pussy?"

"What do you mean? Of course, I do."

"Are you sure?"

More awake now, he props himself on an elbow to face her.

"Why would you ask that?" Sillyboi drags a finger across Chloe's face, which, washed clean of makeup, bares flawless skin.

"It's not, like, weird to you or something?" Chloe looks down at her legs and picks lint off her kneecap covered completely by a tattoo of a blooming gardenia.

"Oh, baby, no! Not at all. Why would you think that?" Sillyboi's hand drops to cup her breast clothed in a pink-camouflage t-shirt.

"This is so embarrassing."

"Tell me."

"I don't know, there is just, like, more…skin hanging

down there than there used to be. You must have noticed."

"What, no! I haven't."

"Silly. Don't lie. You've noticed. There is."

"I mean, if that is true, and I'm not saying it is, it's totally normal."

"I know."

"Baby, no. I never think about it."

"I don't like it though."

"Oh. Baby. I love your pussy, sweetheart. It's the sweetest, most perfect, little pussy in the whole world."

"You know what I'm talking about. It's gotten, like, longer."

"Really?"

"It has."

"Oh."

"I was looking up labiaplasty, yesterday, at work."

Sillyboi laughs.

"Don't laugh."

"I'm sorry."

"They can fix it, but it costs, like, five-thousand dollars." Sillyboi wonders what she might look like with an unlimited budget for surgery. Her ass swells in his imagination.

"Oh, sweetheart, you don't need that."

"For a second, I almost didn't want you to look at my phone."

"What?"

"I almost didn't want to let you look at my phone because I didn't want you to see I'd been googling labiaplasty."

Sillyboi and Chloe's noses touch.

"I love your pussy, baby."

"You do?"

"So much it's literally insane. I think about it all day long."

"No, you don't."

"I do."

"I think about your cock all day long."

"Yeah?"

"Your beautiful cock, yes." Chloe grabs it, thin and lifeless.

Sillyboi kisses Chloe's nose.

"You don't need labiaplasty, my gorgeous. You're perfect. You're the sweetest, most adorable, sexiest girl on the planet." Sillyboi feels his nose itch.

Chloe breathes deeply.

"Silly."

"Yes."

"I'm sorry I made you give me your phone."

"That's okay, baby."

"I shouldn't have."

"It's really okay."

"It was annoying."

"It's okay."

"Ok."

"I love you so much, sweet baby."

"I love you too, Silly."

SIX

(Life is love! Life is love! We must spread love. I can't imagine a better way to champion love than continue this relatable, relevant, and inclusive story of love!)

Sillyboi wakes and is seized by anxiety. It is Monday at 8 a.m. He grabs his phone, opens Instagram, and scrolls, feeling as though a theatrical scrim of fog and filth is separating his consciousness from his thoughts. Sillyboi knows his condition—a consequence of the amount of marijuana inhaled each night—will improve gradually throughout the day and, in a few hours, his senses will grind back to sharpness. But, noticing the scrim and the sensation his muscles have lost their connectivity, a sense of dread overwhelms him.

Today will be my last day smoking weed, is the thought Sillyboi has every morning, at this moment, retarded by reefer. *A cup of coffee will fix me*. Thinking of coffee—another substance enslaving him—leads to the conclusion the best combination for the day, or any day, is caffeine plus THC. *Weed to crack your heart wide open and coffee to eliminate the drowsiness. One cannot ignore the health benefits of an open heart, your honor!*

Sillyboi glances at the half-smoked joint on the side table and is tempted to relight. *Oh, the possibilities of being stoned in daylight!* Sillyboi stiffens his hands to his sides. Monday is an opportunity to make good on the failures of the weekend, which transpired, once again, without making progress on his screenplay.

For Sillyboi, acting is a bipolar profession. Long periods of inactivity punctuated by sporadic bursts, mostly of failure, but sometimes of the sweetest success known to man. A handful of months, or days, of work a year lucrative enough to support a life of vegetable leisure, or long periods of idle time for an ambitious boy to wrangle himself into rigid discipline and claw his way up the creative hierarchy. The very structure that when talking himself off the metaphysical ledge—the desperate internal monologue where his need for supremacy and success is the ongoing subject—he will claim has no merit. His body feels tight. He needs to stretch. Sillyboi has been neglecting his body, but today will be the start of a new regime of physical and mental betterment. He jumps violently out of bed.

"Where are you going?" Chloe groans, awake.

"I have to start my day."

Sillyboi bolts from the bedroom unaware he sounds defensive.

In the living room, Sillyboi practices yoga. His legs feel brittle passing through sun salutations. His thoughts drift to his work. His screenplay. Sillyboi wanted to write a movie in which he could star, a showcase and a launching pad, cinema as a short fuse to ignite explosive fame, revealing Sillyboi to the world as a lucrative A-lister. An opportunity to flex all of his acting muscles at once, the thespian equivalent of competitive bodybuilding, lubed up with Oscar worthy moments, glittering with award-winning co-stars. With this screenplay, his manifesting mantras would finally pay off. (*I am a genius. I am the best actor of my generation. I am a genius. I am the best actor of my generation*). Infinite rejection becomes heroic lore. Sillyboi knew he must write himself an iconic star vehicle like *Rocky* like *Bananas* like *Garden State* like *Tiny Furniture* like *Yentl* like *Braveheart* like *Good Will Hunting* with Sillyboi's name in every above the line category. Sillyboi would become perfect talent: macho and gamine, aggressive and acquiescent. A modern, loveable, epic, subtle, superhero, softy, with the impossible combination of qualities that made Brando, Dean, Phoenix, and all the sainted white male starlets so sublime. But as soon as he started to write his script *Launching Pad* (he titled the Final Draft document as inside joke and small prayer) he encountered a significant problem. In contriving a story centered on a white ubermensch warrior Sillyboi recognized, with a pang of shame, his screenplay had a quality most charitably described as unintentionally retro.

Sillyboi's first stab at *Launching Pad* centered on a character named "Lad the Bad," a methhead motorcyclist married to his 1957 Showa Cruiser (think lube in the exhaust pipe) who sets off on a journey—with a mute underage prostitute—to find and kill the man who raped and kidnaped his mistress—a stripper sex therapist. In the realm of Sillyboi's flawed conception of himself, he was perfect for the role of Lad. But as he crafted motorcycle chases, barroom brawls, and conferences with Native American mystics, all in service of saving a "bi-racial Asian damsel in distress," Sillyboi noticed the story had no "contemporary relevance," two words he wrote in marker on ripped paper and taped to his laptop for inspiration. The screenplay was criminally sexist: a man and child prostitute on a mission to track down the defiler of a weak woman who only appears in the opening rape scene. And the context—white supremacist motorcycle gangs conferring with indigenous people in a fantasy Southwest Sillyboi had neither visited nor was prepared to research—was racist and naïve. Sillyboi, criminal, racist, sexist, and naive in his first attempt, found himself writing dialogue with dated lingo like a 50's throwback. And if there was anything Sillyboi hated, it was nostalgia.

The next iteration of *Launching Pad* Version 2.0 was far more promising. Overcompensating for the sins of his first attempt, Sillyboi set the second draft in 2060, in a world decimated by climate change. To make production possible on a micro-budget, Sillyboi decided to convey inundated earth in a public indoor pool using green screen and low-fi animation to create whimsical post-apocalyptic backgrounds. Sillyboi thrilled at the idea of an indoor public pool as movie studio. A choice rich in allegory. "Indoor" qua womb evoking our dependence (on fossil fuels) and "public"—with ordinary present-day swimmers doing anachronistic laps around the futuristic action—a metaphor for our failure to liberate the working class. Voilà, the film critiques late-capitalism and saves the planet! This, Sillyboi was sure people wanted. *Launching Pad* Version 2.0 was beginning to feel really special.

Sillyboi, still practicing yoga, increases the pace of his sun salutations and remembers the inciting incident of *Launching Pad* Version 2.0: a climate change flood that wipes out 99 percent of the world's population leaving only good people who want to self-improve. All the evil 'isms and phobias are over. Survivors of the flood have one aim: to build peaceful interconnected communities on rafts woven from discarded iPads and iPhones. This would be the first film without conflict. There would be no villain or even minor antagonist. Every member of the diverse cast of characters would be the main character who share the same ethical beliefs, and use up-to-date sensitive language and phrases. Sillyboi was stoked. Finally, a good idea that did good, and spread love. After a manic burst of screenwriting, Sillyboi crashed into the obvious. Imagine you are Mark Zuckerberg mining the data of every liberal in New York and Los Angeles in the year 2015, compiling the most frequent buzzwords on those profiles to train an Artificial Intelligence that writes feature film screenplays. Sillyboi's *Launching Pad* Version 2.0 was way worse than what that program would have written. And, worse than way worse, it had no star-making role for Sillyboi. The very concept of "star-making role" was antithetical to the movie's mission. Realizing his mistake, Sillyboi quit Final Draft, moved *Launching Pad* Version 2.0.fdx to the trash, emptied it, and was immediately overwhelmed with grief. His lost *Launching Pad* wasn't that bad! Sillyboi spent weeks attempting to make it interesting! He coined many new words that each meant "you're valid." In the opening set-piece, his dozen equally important main characters worked together to find innovative ways to apologize. Puppet shows of "I'm sorry," Gregorian chants of "I'm sorry," podcasts of "I'm sorry," rap battles of "I'm sorry," lectures of "I'm sorry," followed by question-and-answer periods of "I'm sorry." Sillyboi imagined ending the movie with a credit sequence that listed a charitable organization the audience could support next to each name credited. Even if the screenplay was never produced, it certainly would have been published in Sillyboi's *Complete Works* after his life's tune changed to the key of permanent success. Sillyboi's future fans would have lined up for the opportunity to discover the brilliant but juvenile antecedents of gestures that would later make his mature masterpieces.

Sillyboi let out the kind of strangled groan that resolves reluctantly into laughter.

"I'm sorry," Sillyboi whispered to himself like the protagonist in a mediocre film. "I'm sorry," he said again.

And then the tears came.

Sillyboi feels Chloe's steps, heavy on the floor behind him, as he suffers through Virabhadrasana, warrior pose, doing his best to take on some of the qualities of the warrior. Chloe sighs with an unmistakable edge, as she passes by him wearing nothing but tattoos on her way to the bathroom, announcing her frustration with a partner who will jump out of bed so quickly for the maintenance of his body, but will not linger for the maintenance of his relationship.

The pain in Sillyboi's thighs is too intense. He drops into child's pose.

Chloe slams the bathroom door.

After a moment that is too brief for any satisfying release, Chloe emerges from the bathroom and offers a weak "hello" as she passes him, his face to the floor, on her way back to bed. Sillyboi knows this is his cue to attend to her. A cue that, if left unanswered, will plague the rest of the day. Sillyboi smells his body odor on the toxic yoga mat one more time before getting up to stand in their bedroom where Chloe is laying, over the covers, phone to her face, short staccato bursts of noise coming from its tiny invisible speakers.

"What is that?" He asks.

"Snapchat."

"You're on that now?"

"I don't post."

"Oh."

"Does it bother you when I do yoga?" It's a dumb question Sillyboi knows he shouldn't be asking. Chloe refuses to look at him.

"Why do you think it bothers me?"

"I don't know but you, like, sighed really loud as I was doing it just now."

"It doesn't bother me."

"Okay." Sillyboi is unconvinced but must get back to *Launching Pad*. So, Version 2.0 was a failure. So what? Today is a new beginning. Sillyboi steps into the middle room of their railroad, small, dark, and outfitted to serve as Chloe's studio, where he keeps a small desk accumulating unread books. The room is also home to their dresser. Sillyboi pulls on his uniform: black Dickies work pants, extra-large white Hanes t-shirt, and triple extra-large black Champion zip-up hoodie. He is almost dressed when Chloe saunters into the room, energy at an all-time low, pulls a matching enormous hoodie from the floor, dons it like a cape, and sits at her desk to begin the slow painterly process of putting on eyeliner and brow pencil.

"Where are you going?" Chloe asks, eyes on her mirror, in a tone contrived to sound as neutral as possible.

"I have to write." Sillyboi says. The statement hangs in the air like a body from a tree.

"I thought we were getting breakfast." Chloe says.

Sillyboi doesn't respond.

"Did you forget that's what we planned?"

"No. I didn't forget. Of course, we're getting breakfast. But can we go soon? I can't waste the entire morning."

Chloe grabs a translucent pink bong on her desk and relights the half-scorched bowl taking a decadent drag. She sucks another chest full of smoke pretending not to notice the hot waves of judgment rising from Sillyboi.

Chloe inspects her face. None of the markings of age are visible, but still, she applies a thick layer of foundation over her freckles. *I'm the most beautiful I'll ever be and I don't even care. That's my privilege,* Chloe thinks, as Sillyboi sits, legs splayed angrily in front of him, on a folding chair next to her desk. A long moment of silence as she pencils her eyebrows and absorbs his anxiety with perverse pleasure, calming her until, eyebrows complete, she speaks.

"Don't worry. I won't be long."

"That's okay." Now it is Sillyboi's turn to flatten his

tone into neutral. It isn't working. "Are you mad at me?" he asks.

"No."

"I think you are."

"You don't know what I am thinking."

"I know. You just seem upset."

"I'm really not."

"Do you think I forgot we had breakfast plans?"

"No."

"I didn't forget."

"Okay, Silly."

Sillyboi looks at the bong and contemplates taking a hit. He pries a fresh nugget of weed from the plastic cube on the desk.

"There's weed already in there." Chloe says, annoyed.

"I'd like some fresh." Sillyboi pinches apart a nugget of weed and adds it to the ashy bowl. "I love weed," he says and takes a deep drag.

"No, you don't."

He exhales.

"What's that supposed to mean?"

"Nothing. You love weed! Of course, you love weed."

"Can we put some music on?"

"I don't care. What?"

"Future?"

"No."

"One song!"

"You have to stop listening to Future."

"Why?"

"It's not good."

"Like, not cool anymore? I don't care about that. *Dirty Sprite 2* is one of the best albums of all time. It's a masterpiece. I'll be listening to Future when I'm seventy!"

"I'm not saying it's not cool. I don't care if it's cool or not cool. I'm saying it's bad for you."

"How is it bad for you?"

"It's catchy, but do you actually listen to what he's saying?

"You can't take it at face-value! There's symbolic weight underneath the lyrics!"

"You're wrong. There's no symbolism. That's the point, actually. It's all right there. It's about drinking codeine, abusing prescription drugs, and mistreating women. It's really violent to women, actually. It's really awful the way he talks about women. It's not good to listen to that kind of thing constantly. It's stupid. It will rot your brain and make you stupid." Sillyboi takes another hit as Chloe continues, "It's propaganda for a really fucked-up way of life. I like the beats too, but that's, like, I mean that's all it is. Honestly, it's fucked-up to listen to that stuff constantly."

"I don't listen to it constantly."

Chloe doesn't respond.

"I don't. Just so you know. Yeah, I get that if you tune into what he's saying it's morally a little repellent. But, at the end of the day, I don't think it's meant to be taken seriously. It's interesting for the symbolic content. Future is living his life as the personification of the id, you know? He embodies the desire to live in excess, in a self-generated spotlight. He's living everyone's wildest fantasies!"

"Men are pigs."

"What? Why are you saying that?"

"All you boys. All you want to do is fuck everything you see."

"That's not true."

"It is."

"I knew you were mad at me! You've been mad at me since the moment we woke up!"

"That's impossible. We didn't wake up together. You woke up, like, stressed out of your mind."

"See! Just because I got up before you doesn't mean I was stressed out of my mind! I wanted to do some yoga and start my day, is that a crime?"

"Is it a crime I don't agree with you about Future? We are allowed to have different opinions! I think he's disgusting. And you don't! That's fine."

"I would never dream of being prescriptive about what you listen to!"

"I'm not being prescriptive!"

"You are! I agree it's fucked how Future talks about women. And, if he actually does as many drugs as he says he does, he's a sad addict who's going to die a tragic death! But I hate maudlin white people music! I refuse to listen to fucking singer songwriter John Mayer, I had a bad day, let me strum my guitar and sing about my cat collection! I have enough sad white person shit going on in my own personality! Future is uplifting! His songs are joyous to me! I don't care what anyone thinks about his lyrics! What's important to me is the emotional content underneath the lyrics and that is joy! Pure joy!"

Chloe slaps the eyebrow pencil down hard on her desk

and moves to the dresser to pull on a pair of black leggings with holes fabricated in the knees.

"That is exactly what worries me about you Sillyboi."

"What do you mean, worries you?"

Chloe drops the sweatshirt and pulls a black sports bra over her head.

"Why I can't trust you."

"What are you talking about?"

"Nothing. Can we please just be quiet?"

"You can't say something like that. That's a bomb. Saying I can't trust you and following it with 'let's be quiet?' That's, like," Sillyboi laughs, "like, literally nuking Times Square and being, like, oh cool, guess no one was hurt!"

"Jesus, Sillyboi! That's not funny! I just want to be quiet! Can you give me that!? Please!?" Chloe finds her t-shirt—black, and five-times extra-large, like a long shapeless dress—grabs a thick leather choker from the top of the dresser—cluttered with makeup, jewelry, tattoo needles, and receipts—and fastens it around her neck with a heavy ornamental lock.

"You get like this when you're stoned," she says calmly.

Rage ignites heat under his skin. *"You yell at me one more time…"* Sillyboi hears Chloe's empty ultimatum from a past argument, and recalling it raises his temperature. Sillyboi argues with the part of her he has internalized. *You're not mad at me, Chloe, you're mad at your parents for abusing you! You provoke me, you compel those around you toward abuse! You're a magnet for abuse!* But Sillyboi keeps this inside, doing everything in his power not to explode. She brushes past him on her way to the front door next to which their shoes are strewn in a chaotic pile. Sillyboi screams without sound and slams his fists into his chest before slapping himself once, twice, three times in the face. He is calm.

"What did you do?" Chloe asks from the other room.

"What?" He asks, as physical pain relieves his pain.

"Are you okay?"

Sillyboi walks into the living room toward their pile of shoes where Chloe sits stoic, zipping platform Docs.

"Silly?"

"Yes, baby?"

Chloe inhales to speak but mutes the impulse.

"What?" he asks, but seeing her expression, is relieved of the desire to hear her response.

SEVEN

At the shop, Chloe does her chores faster than usual, eager to dispel the rising pain in her heart. Breakfast with Sillyboi transpired as usual: egg sandwiches, coffee, and the kind of uninspired chatter punctuated by flights of scrolling that goes on between couples who no longer feel the need to impress each other by dressing up life stories to sound heroic or damaged. Chloe and Sillyboi eat egg sandwiches with the familiarity of people who have tasted each other's asshole. In the middle of that nothing, it almost happened. She was close. The first hot syllables of revelation were on her tongue. But without noticing where her decision to renege on the promise she had made hours before—the decision to reveal her findings and out him—she stifled her whistleblower's impulse and replaced her vitriol with egg sandwich.

Last night, she did what she had not previously allowed herself to do. After Sillyboi fell asleep, she took his phone, unplugged it from its charger, entered his passcode (1,2,3,4) and searched through his texts. After scrolling past conversations with his mother, his father, his sister—and a few unfamiliar names that deeper investigation revealed to be insignificant—Chloe found the thread she was looking for: Sillyboi's correspondence with Celeste. The thread was long. Communication with any girl was inappropriate in Chloe's opinion. But after scrolling through pages and pages of texts, Chloe found, to her enormous surprise, absolutely nothing incriminating.

Chloe was perplexed. There were no explicit photos. There was no flirtation. There was nothing even a mind such as hers, poisoned by suspicion, could interpret as incriminating. Sillyboi and Celeste's conversations were so banal—exchanging criticisms of the director they were working with, interactions about logistics, and a few tepid exchanges about the screenplays they were writing—that, eventually, after a slow day at the shop gave her the space to dissect and transform banality to its inverse, Chloe, in the insecure realm where intuition pursues proof, became committed to the idea something secretive was, in fact, going on between Sillyboi and that girl. It was lurking in the unseen space, the texts not sent, what couldn't be said in those pages and pages and pages of pointless dialogue.

Chloe read the entire text history of Sillyboi and Celeste three times in a row before moving on to look deeper into the bowels of his phone.

The next thread Chloe investigated was between Sillyboi and his psychoanalyst. To come across his analyst's first and last name in Sillyboi's text history, and to see no effort had been made to conceal his identity with an alias, as she absolutely would have done if she had an analyst with whom she regularly texted and divulged her most intimate thoughts and feelings, filled her with an unexpected rush of love for Sillyboi and his trusting naiveté. Chloe steeled herself for what she expected to find: litanies of criticism against her, all the resentments Sillyboi harbors, the countless issues he would never directly share. With her finger poised over the thread—the only text visible from the analyst to Sillyboi reading "I absolutely hear you"—to click and reveal their conversations, Chloe anticipated the most damning revelations, her worst fears confirmed: he doesn't love me, our relationship is meaningless, he thinks I'm a moron, etc. Hurt mutating into anger, Chloe opened the thread with a sharp tap.

The first ten pages of texts Chloe scrolled had to do with Sillyboi's anxiety around his work; paragraphs illustrating the myriad variations on creative frustration:

Another terrible day to add to what feels like an endless and unending cycle of terrible days. I have come to the conclusion I will never be a successful artist. Real artists have struggled. I haven't. All I do is feel anxious about success and live in relative comfort, complaining to you, Chloe, or my parents. If only I had a story to tell, something real or dangerous, something that spoke to a relevant struggle. If only I was Black or a woman or gay, or all three. I am doomed. And, as far as acting is concerned, I know the ship has sailed in that department. I will never be a movie star. And what is terrible is I know I deserve to be one! Horrifying to realize the innocent dreams of youth are slowly disintegrating into...

Chloe kept scrolling through more of the same, stunned by the enormous quantity of whining. Sillyboi's texts to his analyst: the *My Struggle* of pathetic self-evisceration. To read them, you would believe Sillyboi's life was constant pain caused by acute and chronic grandiosity and pretension. Disgust flooded her every organ. How could she be in a relationship with someone so shallow and narcissistic who seemed to value personal success above everything else? How could she reconcile that while she sat at work all day, thinking of him and their relationship—excited when Sillyboi was attentive, devastated when he was distant—he can jump out of bed to his day of anxiety and self-obsession, forgetting to fold his body into hers, kiss her forehead, and inaugurate the day with even the most basic display of affection? How is it possible to live with someone and exist as a mirror in their presence, a reflective surface to remind the other of the flawed self, the desperate and hungry self, always unsatisfied? *Where is the one text about me*, Chloe wondered, *where is the one mention of my existence?* This diagnosis was more damning than infidelity. Nothing is more painful than proof of apathy. *What am I to Silly,* Chloe wondered, *flesh to fuck, a source of love to soothe whenever it's convenient?*

And, just as Chloe was about to quit scrolling and submit to another sleepless night, she found what she was looking for: a small paragraph following a long series of laments—accompanied by relevant photos from many angles —on Sillyboi's hairline and the pain at losing a millimeter, or less, from his temples.

That girl I fucked at SXSW just texted asking if she could build me a website. Build me a fucking website? Is she out of her mind? We haven't even spoken since. Of course, I didn't respond. See, this is why I shouldn't cheat. You run the risk of getting a text like this. What if Chloe had been looking over my shoulder or something?

And there it was. "What if Chloe had been looking over my shoulder or something?" The first mention of her. Her stomach relaxed, her breath became deep, the muscles around her heart released, and from the bottom of her groin a pleasant rush of energy surged. She was not angry. This was true relief. The months of anguish were over. Chloe was not incorrect to be in a constant state of imbalance. She was not wrong to question her sanity. This is what vindication felt like. Calm. Her consciousness rose to a place over her head. She watched her fingers return Sillyboi's phone to the home screen—decidedly not a photo of her—and plugged it back into the outlet to charge. Chloe lay back down, next to Sillyboi, a known philanderer, and fell asleep without trouble.

•

It was two years ago that Sillyboi attended SXSW with an independent film. He played a small but significant role. The film got positive reviews, but critics didn't mention Sillyboi. She remembers him texting about being ignored and feeling resentful. She remembers trying to comfort him, assuring him it was still an honor to be in any film accepted to any film festival. Chloe remembers texting Sillyboi she loved him and Sillyboi texting he loved her back. Since that trip, Chloe and Sillyboi broke up, got back together, and broke up again, before getting back together last summer and finding the apartment where they live now. Chloe can acknowledge time has passed and that the infidelity occurred in a different iteration of their relationship. But the fact remains, Sillyboi had betrayed her. Chloe could sense something was different when he got back from that trip. She suspected he had been unfaithful. *How could it not have happened*, she thought, *a handsome young man, in the limelight, away from his girlfriend for the first time*? But the relationship was new then and Chloe decided to use all her energy to push these thoughts from her mind. She was aware that even the accusation of infidelity could bring a stifling air of tension into a relationship. She and Sillyboi were breathing so deeply then; their rhythm was one of so much laughter and fun, getting stoned, watching YouTube videos, eating fresh fruit, and fucking. And yet, she still felt the need to impress him. Seven years her senior, she looked up to him. No, she could not have him thinking she was a girl who couldn't handle him going away to a film festival, to celebrate his success and career, and come home to a girlfriend full of doubts and accusations. And so, when Sillyboi returned from Austin into her arms, even though he appeared joyful, excited to see her, to kiss her, to laugh with her, her breath became tight and short as if disaster had been transposed over their scene of romantic bliss. But she marshaled her will and smiled till her face hurt. No, nothing was going to ruin the moment of their reunion, certainly not Chloe herself.

It was two years after this first moment of suspicion, when Sillyboi returned from acting in another independent film, this time with a mysterious brunette co-star—petite, pale, full lips—who Chloe knew from one photo on Instagram in which she was tagged with Sillyboi and another non-threatening girl, their arms draped around each other in a moment that either depicted ordinary friendship or concealed erotic tension. Celeste Scott was the girl's name and she had three times as many followers as Chloe on Instagram. This was the image Chloe feared the most: round face, wide-set eyes, plump cheeks, ample behind. She looked like an alternate reality version of herself. And, from that moment, Chloe could see Sillyboi's fall, in slow motion, upside-down, body released to fate.

Chloe took a screenshot of the photo and texted it to Sillyboi.

Who the fuck is this?

A full hour and a half later, Sillyboi responded.

An actress in the film. Why are you worried?

Chloe didn't want to push the subject, but alone in their apartment with nothing but Sillyboi's objects, inanimate and cold, and the Ikea furniture he bought, piney still with the aroma of cheap materials, Chloe could not mitigate her anger, and began to text.

I saw this photo and my stomach fucking dropped out of my ass, Silly. This is not cool, okay?

The release of adrenaline followed by the torture of blinking ellipses, appearing and disappearing, as he drafted and revised his response.

"Say something!" Chloe screamed into the stoned emptiness of her evening damned by suspicion.

Nicole, of course, heard her scream, and turned on *The Bachelor* at full volume. "White cunt!" Nicole shouted, "White cunt," she said again, for emphasis.

Sillyboi's delayed response was the confirmation Chloe needed. Lies need crafting. The truth is quick.

Why aren't you responding? Chloe texted, during Sillboi's ellipses, to force the truth from his fingertips and onto the screen.

Hold on I'm shooting

Chloe tossed her phone on the bed and went to roll a joint with pure sativa, Maui Wowie, which she purchased from one of the tall skinny, backpacked boys who deliver the plastic containers of weed to their apartment. And, as Chloe rolled herself a joint, she willed herself to forget about the photo of Celeste and Sillyboi and focus her attention on a painting she was making of a rosary draped around a pair of roses. The rose was Chloe's favorite subject and she knew she could master reproducing them, with paint or ink, on paper, even if she could never become the master of herself or the erratic behavior of the people in her life. Chloe put the flame to the tip of the joint and the small twist of excess paper combusted into smoke. Chloe inhaled and the cherry burned red, feeling momentarily resolved.

Sillyboi's text would come in soon, a vehement absolution of blame. *I will know,* Chloe thought, *if there is ever real cause for concern, but for now, I must focus on my ink and roses*. Her anxiety slowly dissolved. But, from the moment Sillyboi and Celeste Scott appeared on Instagram together, a malignancy began to grow in the spine of their relationship and Chloe's thoughts were once again perforated by constant incisions into the foundation of her trust.

•

In the shop, chores complete and on her way back from the dumpsters, Chloe is curious why she isn't sobbing, tearing her hair out, and consumed by rage? Why isn't she calling him or sending a litany of texts? She tosses her rubber gloves into one of the empty trash bins as graphic imagery of Sillyboi and Celeste shuffle through her imagination—Sillyboi showing Celeste an expression she thought only for her: saliva coming out of his mouth and into her mouth. If it happened once with some unknown woman, her name not even worth mentioning to the psychoanalyst, it certainly could have happened with Celeste.

At the front desk, Chloe is surprised to see two people sitting on the couch, waiting to be received by an employee. She admonishes herself for neglecting to lock the front door.

One of them approaches.

"Hi." Standing in front of Chloe are two soft boys with light brown skin and eyes that move hesitantly over her and around the room. It takes a moment for Chloe to register that the two visitors share a quality she has never encountered before in shop clientele: Down syndrome. Chloe looks around the empty shop. She is alone. Otis and the other artists won't arrive for hours. Chloe is the only one present. She suppresses a nervous laugh.

"Hey, what can I help you with?" Chloe asks, doing her best to pretend nothing is out of the ordinary. *Is there a rule against tattooing a person with Down syndrome?* Chloe feels the impulse to google the issue but decides against it. *These boys are used to being rejected,* she thinks, *I am not going to act like everyone else.* One of the boys lingers behind the other, shuffling from side to side, suppressing laughter. The boy standing in front does the talking.

"We want tattoos."

Chloe studies the alpha boy's face; a soft strip of down outlines his upper lip, hair that has never seen a razor's edge. These are kids, she realizes, no older than fourteen.

"Sure, I have to see some IDs first, though." The alpha looks back to the beta whose smile disappears into quivering uneasiness.

"We don't got 'em."

"I'm sorry, then. I can't tattoo you without IDs."

"We're eighteen."

"I'm sure you are. But it doesn't matter how old you are, I can't legally tattoo you unless you present me with some form of identification."

"Please!" Alpha is suddenly desperate, placing his hands down hard on the front desk with the full weight of his torso on his wrists and his face tilted to an impossible angle: chin to the ceiling, head tilted sideways toward the floor into such an extreme posture of entreaty, he appears as a figure from an ancient painting, when to desire strongly was to let it shape you.

"It's our only chance! We need tattoos!" Alpha says, cracking into hysterical falsetto. Chloe looks at Beta shuffling nervously behind him. Beta looks out the shop's front window to see if they are being watched or followed.

"I'm sorry," Chloe says as her phone vibrates in her pocket, "I can't do it without IDs. Why don't you run home and get them?"

"We can't." Alpha says.

"I don't know what to tell you then man."

"You don't want to do it!" Alpha says, his anger increasing.

"I'm sorry." Chloe replies, getting defensive.

"You just don't like us." Alpha is on the verge of tears.

"What?" Chloe looks around for backup. There is none. "That's not it at all! I just don't want to get in trouble!"

"You hate us!"

"Please go! I don't want to have to call the cops."

"You're a retard hater!"

"What!?"

"RETARD HATER!!" Alpha screams at the top of lungs, grabs Beta, and storms out. Chloe grabs her phone. The text is from Sillyboi.

I'm sorry about this morning, baby. I really need to work on myself and my tendency to let my anxiety get in the way of enjoying a beautiful morning with the girl I adore more than anyone else in the entire world. I love you so fucking much. I am so proud of you. You are killing it baby. Please send me a picture if you do any walk-ins today. Your work fills me with inspiration! Love you so much.

Chloe doesn't respond.

EIGHT

Sillyboi sits in a cafe, dense with freelancers, at his laptop, so the bright light of the blank page might penetrate his psyche and scrape out a shred of latent genius: like Ivan slipping on peel after peel of virality, or Ms. Slow Death popping from self-tapes into the hearts and pocketbooks of producers. Sillyboi fingers his keyboard, paralyzed. He is confident both versions of *Launching Pad* were bad, flitting between flaccid extremes: offensive or anodyne to the point of failure. His entire essence feels anti-cinematic. Self-sabotaging stock questions stifle him: *wouldn't it be better for society, as a privileged straight white man, to quit personal art and promote under-privileged artists?* What from his experience could ever become cinema? Sillyboi's only trauma was premature birth. He self-soothes, thinking about Instagram. *Who's my most valuable follower*, Sillyboi wonders? *Duh, it's Ryder Ripps. What's wrong with extremes? Ryder is extreme.* Sillyboi googles Ryder, a straight white man who hired Craigslist hookers to doodle on Ace Hotel stationary and sold them at Sotheby's; who screenshotted 300K follower model Adrianne Ho's posts, and paid Jeff Koons' clones to make them six figure price tagged, Photoshop liquified, square for posting, oil paintings. Scanning reams of scathing tweets deriding Ryder, Sillyboi craves extreme attention. Sillyboi opens Instagram to his favorite series of Ryder posts that begin as if a female grad student has taken over his account. She posts her average corny-core law school routine. She posts flying to Syria. She posts attempting humanitarian aid. She posts learning weapons. She posts becoming a mercenary. She posts joining the civil war. In her last post, her pretty face is pale, bloody, and distorted, wrapped in a dusty white fleece and purple lace shroud: dead. Swarms of fans and haters comment flatteries and critiques. "This the height of male privilege," they comment. "Conceptual art to Syria, surreal arc bro," they comment. "Callous," they comment. "I can't stop thinking about this," they comment. Ryder responds to some of the rips. "I'm writing a movie," Ryder says. "Performance art," he says.

One day, I'll have haters, Sillyboi prays, *and when they hate, I'll know I have risked. I'll know I am good. There must be a record of how I was hated and good.* But Sillyboi takes no risk. He needs only love. His back aches. He blames machines. *Must I give my prime to the computer? I belong on stage saying lines I didn't write! If only I could be the last straight white guy to play Hamlet on Broadway!* Sillyboi googles "top grossing broadway shows of 2015," and scrolls to see Kander and Ebb's *Cabaret* still running. Sillyboi groans. *If only I could replace whatever third string twink is currently the Emcee in Cabaret! If only I could be the last straight white guy to win the Oscar for doing drag! If only I could be the last straight white guy to win for being "bad!"*

Sillyboi's phone vibrates with a call from Ivan. He answers, obviously.

"Sillyboy. I did it." Ivan says, and Sillyboi feels him use the old spelling.

"What?"

"Sold a show."

"What? Wow."

"To HBO with this huge, like, insanely huge producer. He saw my videos, loved them, and asked me to write a pilot. So I did. It only took two weeks. I'm a great writer when I sit down to do it. This was three months ago. We've been negotiating the deals ever since. I promised myself I wouldn't tell a soul until every deal was signed. And they all were! Today! So, I'm telling you man!"

"That's actually incredible."

"I know. I'm the lead, and the head writer, and the showrunner. Co-showrunner. They're gonna get a woman of color to do it with me. It's everything I've ever prayed for."

"No one deserves this more than you, Ivan."

"Thank you so much, man. I love you so much, Sillyboy."

"I love you so much, Ivan." Sillyboi feels true love melt the winter in his chest. "I've never had any doubt this would happen for you," Sillyboi continues, imagines gunmetal, and bites down. "What's it about?" he asks, jaw clenched.

"My life. I wrote the absolute truth about everything interesting that's happened to me recently and they love it."

"Wow."

"Same producer as Donald Glover."

"Wow."

"I'm pinching myself."

"You don't have to."

"All my dreams came true."

"How many times do you think you were legitimately destroyed over not booking some pathetic, like, guest star that's literally nothing compared to what you have now, to creating your own show."

"I know."

"You're Donald Dunham, dude."

Ivan laughs. "My final form, Black Israelite female faggot."

Sillyboi laughs, "exactly."

"You've always seen me Sillyboy. After drama school, when no one would sign me, you were the only person in my life who told me not to worry. You were so confident. Remember? You said, 'One day, Ivan, they'll be begging you to make them a masterpiece.' Remember? You said that! Remember?"

Sillyboi laughs, "I do."

"You've always seen what I've always been, an all-the-way-to-the-sun-and-back-superstar genius."

"I did. I still do. It's so cool."

"It's the coolest."

Sillyboi imagines murdering Ivan and himself: ending his futile efforts and Ivan's effortless genius. All the rage of mankind is in Sillyboi. Heaven has no rage like success to failure turned, nor hell a fury like a frustrated artist. *If only*

Hitler had been accepted to art school! Sillyboi thinks, imagining himself Hitler and Ivan the Jews. *I'm sorry Ivan. I love you so much. I just need one less genius on earth to compete with. How does Ivan succeed being honest? How does Ryder succeed being fake? I must be more honest,* Sillyboi thinks. *No, fuck it, actually, I should be fake! I must find my art that is honest and fake, to be risky and bad and loved and hated and good!*

NINE

At four-thirty, Otis arrives at the shop, expressionless. But Chloe can detect a bad mood in an Asian man. He walks past her and retreats to the closet that functions as a private office, large enough to stock miscellaneous items: old t-shirts with the shop's logo, books, a bike frame, and a card table for rolling blunts.

The shop is busy. Four girlfriends from Long Island on a "Bushwick street-art tour" came in on a whim to get matching "steak tattoos" in honor of their new commitment to a strict "paleo" diet. Sean—a senior tattooer who hides his hair loss and hangovers with a small cap and smirk and whose lines fall out despite a decade of tattooing—is tracing the basic steaks. No shading, as the girls requested; their reference a clip-art rib eye found on Pinterest. Sean tried to convince Chloe to lighten his load and take on two of the steaks, but the girls demanded the same artist apply them all "so they, like, match perfectly, you know?" Sean, strapped for cash, conceded to stupid tattoos.

Chloe, still at the front desk, is redrawing a Sailor Jerry

pin-up, making her over with pleasers, fishnets, acrylics, hoops, and a wad of cash held to her ear like a phone, when Otis emerges from the closet and motions for Chloe to join him outside. At the thermal copier, waiting for the steak stencils to emerge, Sean groans with jealousy as he whiffs the blunt in Otis's hand.

"Fuck you guys," Sean says.

"Snooze, you lose," says Otis.

"I'm tattooing steaks on anorexics!" Sean whispers loud enough for everyone to hear. Chloe and Otis leave Sean with the girls from Long Island, high on starvation and the defining moment of their friendship.

Seated at tables in the courtyard adjacent to Super Happy Tattoo, people under thirty-five (in 2012, I would have called them "hipsters," in 2015, "Health Goth," and some are evidence "Sea Punk" did not die in 2011) are absorbed by their laptops and phones. Chloe glances over the shoulder of a young man with a light blue crew cut wearing a black Adidas tracksuit under a white faux-fur coat (the missing link between "Sea Punk" and "Health Goth" perhaps) and notices his screen is cluttered with Facebook chats. Otis sits in his usual spot on the ledge of a planter ten yards from the cluster of freelancing creatives. Chloe knows Otis wants to talk or else he wouldn't have invited her outside. Otis lights the blunt and inhales three times before passing it to Chloe who tastes the smoke spiced with a touch of wax.

"What's up?" Chloe asks.

"I didn't get to sleep till, like, four-thirty last night."

"That sucks."

"It's normal for me."

"I'm also having trouble sleeping."

"After midnight, my mind gets so fucking active. Which is good. I watched ten episodes of *Louie* last night." (Oh, how we loved Louie without reservation! The pope of perversity! The sheik of the unsayable! So he jerked off in front of … I just inhaled cannabis myself, so excuse what I am about to say—how could I not partake of the plant while Chloe and Otis are enjoying theirs—as I try to remember something said by a superior mind on this subject —why must everything remind me of my inferiority! My sweet grandiosity how I long for thee! The new perversity is traditionalism. The new perversity is fundamentalism. Vanity is not perverse. Queerness is not perverse. The new perversity is not exhibitionism. I love Louis, even now, in exile. Louis was the final boss. The last important straight white man in culture. The last libtard alpha. There will be no others. We, straight white American men, grew up wondering how we got so lucky to be born this way. We had pulled the trump card from life's deck. But children neglect analysis. We did not seek to know why we had been born on top. The highest place from which to fall, and fall we did, we crashed with Louis—millennial men—our eyes now lidded with anxiety, either apologizing and qualifying or raging and spitting. We were brutal in youth. Imagining sticks were rifles and beating our chests, and then, at the dawn of adulthood, we were told to despise our built-in rage, while others—on "the wrong side of history"—as if history ends with an award show and not all-encompassing flames— celebrated theirs. Which side to choose? Must we choose? I remember now. The superior mind said something like this: Louis was the man on top who played the man on bottom. Louis displayed his cock the way he delivered punch lines, hard. In his hotel room, hard, he undid himself, and our perversity, and we who loved him must now shut up and bear this deluge of silence.)

"He's so funny," Chloe replies.

"I've watched the entire series, like, four times or maybe six. And, I was thinking, like, I could do that. I could be the star of my own television show. If someone followed me around with a camera, like, the shit they would capture? Like, the little interactions and the characters that come through here? It could be really interesting. Or, I don't know, I think it could be." Otis says.

"Like a documentary?"

"See that's the thing, it would be made like a documentary, but the way to present it would be more like *Louis*. Just like a show. And the audience wouldn't know whether it was real or fake. I like that kind of thing. It's tense."

"That could be funny." Chloe almost tells Otis about her encounter with the Down's boys earlier but holds back.

"So, my brain was, like, buzzing on this idea, thinking about who I could get to possibly shoot it. Maybe Julio from the bike shop, he likes film and shit, I'm pretty sure, but he's usually busy. My mind was just active. More than usual. The last time I remember looking at the clock, it was, like, five and I was smoking the second half of this joint thinking it might help, but it just got my mind going even more, you know? And then I was thinking about my family and how I haven't seen or spoken to them in over a decade. Well, barely spoken. You know they haven't seen me with a single tattoo?"

"Holy fuck, really?" Chloe is stunned by this revelation. Otis is covered from the bottom of the chin to his feet in tattoos.

"No, why would they? I haven't seen my parents since I was seventeen. I had no tattoos then. But I'm wondering, like, what the fuck would they think if their first interaction with me after all these years was on a television show? How trippy would that be?"

"I bet they would like it."

"What?"

"The show. About you. I would like it."

"That's not the point. The point isn't whether they would like it or not. I can tell you one thing for sure my dad would fucking hate it. He hates anything that doesn't have to do with religion. My mom is the same way but she would probably be charmed for purely sentimental reasons."

"Yeah. I get it."

Otis takes another drag from the blunt, "Fuck Y'all" tattooed on his knuckles in ornate heavy metal script with delicate tendrils of flourish extending all the way to his cuticles.

"I need a girlfriend. I think that's part of the problem. I sleep better when I am with someone. I've been single for too long."

"It hasn't been that long, has it?"

"Eight months? Yeah, that isn't really long. What people don't know about me is I like to be in a relationship.

But my eye always wanders, that's the thing. No matter what. In a relationship. Single. I've got a wandering eye. I look at girls. It gets me in trouble. It got me in trouble with Rachel. But it doesn't mean anything. If I'm in a relationship, I am loyal."

"I have to ease up on Sillyboi."

"Why?"

"I've been really annoying recently."

"Why?"

"I tell you he finally got a tattoo?"

"What?"

"His name on his stomach, huge."

Otis nods.

"Kinda dumb."

"Why are you being annoying?"

"For looking at girls."

"Guys have to do that Chloe. That's just part of being a guy." Chloe wants to mention last night's discovery and repudiate Otis's theory of the harmlessness of the wandering male eye. But, sensing his emotional equilibrium might be even more fragile than her own, she holds her tongue and wonders if her knack for detecting fragility—the alarm that sounds more or less constantly and with everyone—is perception or projection.

"Family shit," Otis repeats himself, "strange how it's been keeping me up at night. That and *Louie*." Otis erupts with a strangled laugh. "I fucking love that guy."

"Sillyboi and I are almost done with season five. So good."

"He's a God. A modern God. Maybe I need to start

playing music again. Violin. I need to branch out. Maybe that's why I'm thinking about this TV show idea. Like, tattooing, for me, it's not enough. I know that's probably hard for you to hear since you're young and new to the game and it probably all feels romantic as fuck still, but you'll see, it gets tiresome. It does. It's a blue-collar job. We're like plumbers here."

"Yeah." Chloe doesn't agree. Chloe knows she will take their craft to heights Otis could never reach. She wants to correct him. To remind him of great tattooers: old masters like Sailor Jerry and Bert Grim. Contemporary masters like Ruebendall and Vargas. New York legends like Scott Campbell, Rich Fie, Bert Krak, Criss Cleen, Tamara: those who have elevated plumbing to art. And if the institutions that govern art never recognize tattooing as art, it is. Or is it? On this point, Chloe remains undecided and laughs at the comparison. Plumbing vs. art: both pass time, exercise the wrist, and process human waste.

"Sometimes, I think this isn't for me." Otis continues, "I love tattooing and I love the shop as a place for people to be and hang out, but I don't know, there could be another life for me after this one. Tattooing might not be the last stop. It might not. I wonder if I should go back home and visit my family. I think about that all the time, you know, I wonder if seeing them might jam something loose in me and might get me to the next idea, the next big plan. Like this shop. It's just one part of the master plan. Part two and three are on their way. Just wait." Otis's smile is mischievous and terrified. "Just you wait." Otis takes another drag and hands the blunt to Chloe who is stoned from one hit.

"What about you," Otis looks to her, "how's your family?"

Suddenly, Chloe realizes she is crying, without sound, eyes leaking, and is embarrassed to be the girl crying at work, but can't stop. She takes another hit from the blunt.

"Not good," Chloe says.

"What's up?"

"It's my mom."

"Uh-huh."

"She fucking cheated on my dad. I just found out. Like a month ago. In the strangest way too, she, like, decided to tell one of my old friends from home. Like, before she even told my dad, she told this girl Kayla Evanston, and Kayla told me in a fucking DM on Instagram. Kayla doesn't even have my number or email. We haven't spoken in, like, three years. We were never even close! But for some reason my mom always thought we were. Seriously, we haven't spoken in three years. This was the first time. Her telling me that my mom is having an affair with one of her co-workers."

"What the fuck?"

"I know. It's fucked."

"She told some random girl? I don't get that."

"Neither do I. It's so weird. She was probably drunk. I guess she thinks we're still friends? She's so sick. She is such a sick psychotic person. They need to get divorced. But you know Chinese men. Too much pride. He never will. They never should have gotten married in the first place. I don't even care that I wouldn't have been born. That woman has caused so much grief for my dad. He should have stayed in China. He would have been happier there. I know it."

"Who knows? Maybe not."

"No. I know. He would be happier there for sure. He's not American. Like, not in any way. He hasn't assimilated. He doesn't want to. He's a fish out of water, still. And now he's stuck with this cheating cunt of an American wife and two white daughters he doesn't understand or relate to. I'm such a disappointment to him. I don't want to be. I want to make him happy. He just doesn't know who I am."

"He never will."

"I know."

"No, Chloe, seriously, you got to fucking let go of that shit right now if you want to be okay."

"He hates me."

"No, he doesn't."

"He hates my tattoos."

"Of course he does. So?"

Chloe is silent.

"Are you going to stop getting them for him?"

"No."

"So, forget about it. My parents will probably have a heart attack when they finally see me."

"How long's it been again?"

"When?"

"Since you've seen them?"

"Fifteen years."

"Maybe that's what I need to do. Just not see them for a decade. My mom is a cunt. My sister is brainwashed. She can't think for herself. It would be too scary if she did. If she questioned anything about them, she would have to question her own choices and that would probably destroy her. I did talk to my mom. I called her after I got the DM from Kayla. I confronted her and she broke down and admitted …" Chloe groans as the image of her mother fucking a faceless man downloads slowly into her brain, obscuring her vision. She makes an effort to distort the image with psychic interference, but this only produces a peculiar texture around the invading obscenity, a kitsch filter laid over the graphic unseeable. "It's so disgusting she was, like, with this guy."

"Do you know him?"

"Of course not."

"Does your dad?"

"I don't know. I hope not for his sake. She claimed it only happened once, which I think is bullshit. And, the strangest part is—and this is a lie, I am telling you, all that woman does is lie, my whole life—I am pretty sure that, like, seventy percent of what she has said to me over the years, or maybe eighty, a large percentage of what she says is fake, or some version of the truth that makes her look slightly better than the garbage person she is."

"Did she do that with this?"

"Oh, yeah, like, she says when it happened, she disassociated or something. She says she doesn't remember doing it. But that's a lie. Of course, she remembers and of course it happened more than once. And, my poor dad, you know, he's so fucking repressed. I told her she had to tell him. That I didn't want to be the one to do it, and she cried like a little bitch and told me I had to. And I was, like, bitch, stop, please, this is your bed, fucking sleep in it. And then the next night she texted me at, like, 3 a.m. and I know she was wasted. When she's drunk, she texts in these, like, small spurts—not in full sentences—so it comes out like, 'I' dot, dot, dot, 'did it,' dot, dot, dot, 'told your father,' on three separate lines like some fucking, I can't even, it's so fucking lame." Chloe takes the blunt from Otis and inhales again. There is no more work to be done today.

"Did you talk to him?"

"I called the next day. He was being super Chinese about it."

"Yeah, I got a Taiwanese dad. I know the drill. I can't believe you even brought it up to him, to tell the truth."

"I had to! He has no one to talk to but me! No one! He doesn't have friends. He only knows people from work! There is no one there he can actually talk to. I tried to get him to talk. I could tell he was, like—oh god, it was horrible —I could tell he was super upset. He kept saying weird shit, like, 'It's fine Chloe, this is for grownups to talk about, not children,' and I'm like 'Dad, I'm not a fucking child anymore!' Which, he won't hear. To him, I'll always be a baby. But, so, I'm, like, 'Dad, so what I'm a child, you need to talk about this! I know what happened!' And he's like, 'She shouldn't have told you.' And, I'm like, 'It doesn't matter at this point what should or shouldn't have happened! I know! I know! So, just talk about it with me! What are you going to do? Are you going to get a divorce?' And he just couldn't hear anything I was saying. He wouldn't respond to me at all. He just kept saying he would 'make it okay,' and then he begged—literally begged—me not to tell my sister, which, I mean, I don't want to tell her, it's not my place to tell her, but also, I couldn't promise him I wouldn't. And, then he started telling me he loved me over and over again in this really sad pathetic tone I had never heard before, and that really freaked me out so I started crying and then he asked me to go back to school and get my degree."

Chloe laughs; so does Otis.

"And, yeah," Chloe continues through laughter, "that made me hate him again!" Suddenly Chloe seizes up, realizing maybe she has talked for too long and humiliated herself, a horrible recurring feeling. She presses her lips together and hopes Otis is still her friend.

"Fuck." Otis says after a long silence.

"Yeah."

"That sucks."

"Mm-hmm."

"Anyway. Sorry."

"Why?"

"For going on and on about this. It's sad. And probably annoying to listen to."

Otis shakes his head.

"It's heavy. It's real shit."

"Yeah."

"You tell Sillyboy?"

"No. Not yet. I will."

"Why haven't you?"

Chloe knows why she hasn't, because to bring up the subject of infidelity would be to trigger the immediate excavation of the corpses moldering in the memory of Sillyboi's phone. Chloe wants to tell Otis about the texts—to find an older male to champion her cause—but decides against it, fearing he might take the male position and admonish her for invading the sanctity of Sillyboi's digital privacy, claiming the revelation null and void, inadmissible in the chaotic domestic court where couples adjudicate their impulses.

"I'll tell him at some point. He's really preoccupied with work. I don't want to burden him."

"Don't think like that."

"No, I know. I'll tell him. That's not really it. I will tell him. I just haven't wanted to yet." Chloe looks down at her hand and notices she has been holding the blunt for an inappropriate amount of time and is too stoned to take another drag.

"Sorry." Chloe hands the blunt back to Otis who is studying the hexagonal cement tiles under their feet. Self-conscious, Chloe looks around and imagines the post-hipster-sea-punk-adjacent-health-goths, still typing away on their laptops and phones, have overheard her story and are now trying to figure out how best to turn what she just said into post-ironic memes re: the futility of male/female relationships for the social media platform on which they have the largest following.

"Family is a funny thing." Otis says, finally, after a pause.

"Yeah," is all Chloe can manage.

"No, what I mean is you have these people in your life, mom, dad, brother, sister, and you're bound to them by blood. Like, the cosmic law of life says you're bonded, and you are. But the way I think about it is true family and blood family are not always the same. True family may not even be the right way of talking about it, actually. Cosmic family. The family that goes through your shit with you isn't always the people you were born to. For some it is, and that's fine, but for many, you have to find your family. Your life's journey can be about finding your new family, you know?"

"Yeah."

"You get what I'm saying?"

"Sort of."

"I'm saying, fuck them. It doesn't matter. We're your family now. The shop is your family. This place is here for you. You found a cosmic family. So, no matter what happens with your blood. It can flow up. Or down. It can even flow out of you, through a wound, like it is right now. Cosmic family stays balanced no matter what, and that's because there isn't the messy polluted nature of blood in the mix. It's cleaner. It can be more buoyant that way."

Chloe feels the urge to sob.

"Thank you for saying that, Otis. That really means a lot to me." Chloe wishes she could say more but the conversation feels concluded. Otis takes the last drag of the blunt, now a small roach, and grinds it to dust under his black and white Adidas slides.

"See what I'm saying?!"

"What?"

"This shit, what's happening right now, this is the kind of conversation that would be good for the documentary or, like, the T.V. show, or whatever."

TEN

At eight-thirty pm, an hour before the shop is scheduled to close, a group of guys enter asking to be tattooed. They wear variations on the same outfit, greasy Carhartt work pants, hoodies with large logos, and windbreakers. Two of the guys carry skateboards. Chloe sits at an empty station, listening to the new Drake album. Chloe sees Otis tell them they are too late to get tattooed. One of the guys explains something with strong gestures that indicate their presence in the shop is solemn and necessary. Even from behind, Chloe can see Otis's posture saying it's not going to work, come back tomorrow, the shop is closed, everyone has gone home. Only the two of them—Chloe and Otis remain, delaying their return to the sleeplessness that awaits them, alone for Otis, and, for Chloe, home to where strong feeling has been replaced by disconcerting hollowness.

Chloe opens Instagram and searches Sillyboi's account. He hasn't posted today.

Otis is standing over her.

"Help me set up my station, okay?"

"Aren't we closed?"

"I'm staying open for these guys. Their best friend killed himself today."

David was only 20. He had a gorgeous girlfriend, a little brother who idolized him, and parents who, married and healthy, hardly ever raised their voices and lived in western Massachusetts. David's hardcore band, Shit Blood, was gearing up to do a five-city East Coast tour after gaining prominence in the New York scene. Life appeared to be going rather well for David until this morning when his oldest and dearest friend, Marty, the drummer of Shit Blood, found him in a bathtub thick with his own blood, wrists cut vertically. He didn't leave a note.

Chloe watches Otis shake his head and mutter condolences. He turns the sign on the front door from "open" to "closed," locks the gate, and puts up the privacy screen to obscure the front window so that forties can be toasted and blunts can be smoked.

David's bandmates decided their memorial tattoo would be a favorite quote of his: "Shred till you're dead." Marty, who met David on the first day of kindergarten when he asked David to teach him how to draw the mysterious symbol—swastika—David was drawing on the clothing of his stick figure army men, is getting the tattoo on his chest. Julian, the lead singer of Shit Blood, who met David in Hebrew school, and who still owes David the four hundred dollars he needed to fund a 17-year-old girl's abortion, is getting the tattoo on the back of his calf. Kyle, who became friends with David in an unlikely fashion, after David started dating his older sister Miranda, is getting the quote on the back of his arm. And, Sammy, the bassist for Shit Blood, is getting the quote on the front of his shin. Chloe reads each name feeling slightly annoyed at the lightness that can come with grief; wishing that her own interpersonal blockage would resolve into catastrophe and grant her the same blissful release displayed by this group of dudes, so present with each other, enjoying life, as one does, in the shadow of unbearable loss.

The last of David's friends is taking a while to hand over his release form. Chloe takes out her phone to text Sillyboi. It is proper, Chloe believes, to inform your boyfriend when you're going to return home later than expected. She begins a text:

hi bb Imma be late at the shop these guys just showed up who...

"Here ya go." A voice disrupts her typing. Chloe looks up to see a face with high cheeks and a thick spray of black curls falling playfully over green eyes. Chloe takes the release form from the hand that belongs to that face—a face difficult not to notice—and glances at the name.

"Thank you." Chloe decides not to say his name, which she now knows is Alex. Alex smiles: dimples frame his large mouth. Chloe deletes her unfinished text.

Grief lifts the mood in the shop even higher than the forty-ounce bottles of malt liquor and extra-large blunt, provided by Otis, as Chloe dutifully sets up his station in anticipation of the four tattoos. The friends reminisce about David as if he might walk through the door at any moment.

Otis decides not to make stencils for the tattoos, opting instead to draw the letters on the body, free hand. The way he imagines David would have wanted them done. The guys, not understanding or giving the process much thought, have no objection. Shirt off, Marty is first in Otis's chair. He has a couple tattoos, a Celtic cross on his chest and a stick-and-poke "MOM" on his forearm. The boys laugh and joke in a way so specific to their group that to be on the outside is to experience an undiscovered dialect. *These boys seem sweet,* Chloe thinks. They remind her of friends she used to make, when she pretended to skate and danced in fuzzy boots at EDM festivals. Chloe raises her cell phone to take a photo of the group, but decides against it, not wanting any evidence on her phone.

Across the room from where Chloe sits, Alex stares at her, bouncing his knee, narrowing his eyes, and doing little to conceal his desire. *This is my place of work, not a bar,* Chloe thinks, *stop looking at me, I'm not for sale. It's only tattoos, bro.*

As if intuiting her thoughts, Alex looks away and stands to address Marty, now under the influence of Otis's machine.

"How's it feel?" Alex asks.

Marty says something unintelligible and Alex laughs with an inauthentic roar before bounding across the room to where Julian sits, closer to Chloe now; each of his movements a calculated flirtation. Chloe holds her phone higher to hide her attraction: a feeling enhanced exponentially by self-criticism.

"What do you think?"

Chloe looks up from scrolling to find Alex smiling in front of her.

"Excuse me?" Chloe says, intending to stop the conversation before it begins.

"Have you ever ridden a horse?" Alex asks. Chloe chooses to hide her confusion.

"Ah, yeah, once, when I was, like, seven."

"Did you like it?"

"I don't really remember, dude."

Alex points at Julian, who buries his face in his hands, flushed with beer and embarrassment.

"Homeboy over there is scared of horses."

"Bro!" Julian protests. "That's not ..." Julian faces Chloe to address her directly. "We were talking about the apocalypse and what we would do if, like, Trump, gets elected and there's suddenly anarchy, right? And, so, Alex said, it could be a good thing, cause, like, the world economy would break down and maybe we would go back to a more primitive and authentic way of life. And, so like, in that scenario, do you imagine people are going to all of a sudden be riding horses instead of cars?"

"Are you actually asking me?" Chloe asks.

"Yeah."

"Probably not, no. I think there would still be cars, even in the apocalypse."

"See, yeah, that's what I said!" Julian says, feeling vindicated, "It's pretty unrealistic to think that when the economy breaks down everyone, for some reason, is going to be awarded their own stallion just because you think the idea is aesthetic or something."

"It's not about aesthetics!" Alex hops up and down, hair bouncing as if loaded with springs at the root of each follicle. "Julian's afraid of horses, he just doesn't want to admit it."

"I admit it!" Julian defends himself directly to Chloe, who is doing her best to display a massive indifference. "I was thrown off one as a kid! I don't like them. I don't like horses! I don't like cops on horses! Dude, stop trying to make this about me, just 'cause you have unrealistic ideas about the future!" Alex laughs. He paces and grazes the top of Chloe's Doc Marten with his Vans. She pretends not to notice.

Another hour passes. Chloe and Sillyboi have still not texted. Julian is the last to get tattooed. Chloe craves a cigarette. She quit for Sillyboi and what does it mean, she wonders, taking on philosophy to pass the time—and distance herself from the boys still frolicking around the shop—to take action for another? Chloe eyes Otis's tobacco resting close to the edge of his desk, grabs the bag, and rolls one.

Back in the courtyard, smoking, partially to punish him for not texting, Chloe observes the dumpsters and wonders if they still contain this morning's garbage. Somewhere inside the dumpsters are bags of bloody paper towels and excess ink, the runoff from yesterday's tattooing, which this morning she deposited there, infecting them. Chloe imagines the wide rectangular containers sprouting legs and lesions to become faceless monstrosities; armless, but with a limitless capacity to consume. She inhales her cigarette and savors the sensation of burning at the back of her throat. Cigarettes are an opportunity to breathe deeply and relish in playful annihilation. The delicate weight of her phone seems to increase in her pocket the longer it sits idle, making subtle but constant demands on her attention. She craves its vibration, the warm friction of contact. Chloe hears footsteps behind her.

"Can I bum one?" Alex asks.

"I rolled this, sorry."

Alex pulls a pack of Marlboro No. 27s from his pocket, discovers his last cigarette, and makes a soft noise to acknowledge his surprise.

"This is cool." Alex says.

Chloe is confused.

"What?"

"That we didn't meet on Tinder."

She laughs.

But Alex doesn't smile. He is without artifice. The entitlement of this boy confounds her. Chloe wants to scream. She wants to hit him. But the thought of hitting him makes her wet.

"You meet a lot of girls off Tinder?" she asks.

"Ah, how should I answer this?"

Chloe rolls her eyes.

"No, honestly, yeah, I used to. I was rebounding pretty hard. But I'm not on it anymore."

"You're not?"

"No."

"You were in a relationship?"

"For two years, yeah."

"That's a while."

"Yeah."

"Sorry it didn't work out. What did you do?"

"She met someone else."

"Oh, sorry." Chloe feels bad for assuming the worst.

"It's okay."

"That sucks."

"It did."

"Everyone says that, you know."

"What?"

"Just got off Tinder, just got on. Can't be true for everyone."

"Oh." Alex laughs. "Yeah. I guess not."

Alex looks down at the concrete tiles, his body emitting the energy of genuine suffering, as Chloe acknowledges, once again, how those who lead with blustery shows of confidence are often the easiest to injure. Chloe looks away and smokes in silence, her focus drifting back to the dumpsters, ten or fifteen yards in front of her; structures built to receive the building's refuse, not so dissimilar from the role she is forced to play, first as the receptacle of Alex's attention, and now, his pain. (And aren't we all full of unprocessed garbage, rotting away, emitting toxic fumes? I am sick. I am not well. When are we getting back to sex? I know what you're thinking and you're thinking about fucking. How could you not be? Why are you reading this book with its cloying title? Likely marketed to you with some smug shade of pastel garnishing the cover. Pastels are everywhere, infantilizing us, wrapping the neoliberal disease in the palatable, capitalism defanged by matte packaging, just add white to saturated pigment and the result is clean, feminine, and easy to consume. I had nothing to do with the design! I assure you! Nothing! Every designer I suggested—and I suggested many underprivileged artists, who would have gained much by the collaboration—were ruthlessly rejected! Yes, it was fucking—hard wet fucking—that brought you to this book. I wonder how critics will appraise my attitude toward sex after this tome lands on the "the new and noteworthy" tables in the chic bookstores in the urban centers? "Clearly the work of an unrepentant sex addict, *Sillyboy* manages to objectify each of its characters in every moment; lousy with latent misogyny, the author evokes the lewd on almost every page but, sadly, not a moment is truly erotic or stimulating." If I were a woman my take would be heralded as "essential," "subversive," and "necessary." Now I remember: in 2012 I had dinner with a competitor—looking back on the incident I would describe the fellow now as "enemy"—and we were chatting about someone he had worked with for years who I knew only from tabloids. I don't remember what preceded my statement, but I remember describing the colleague of my enemy, who I knew only from tabloids, as "hot in a trashy way." My enemy was livid and shamed me for speaking about his cherished friend—a girl who was "like a sister to him"—in such a derogatory mode. So, you see, I am not the virtuous angel you thought I was. I too have skeletons in my closet from 2012. Enough of this, onward! Closer and closer to the sex you crave!)

"What's wrong with the girls on Tinder?" Chloe unintentionally gives voice to a thought.

Alex is surprised to hear Chloe rejoin the conversation

and his expression reestablishes itself from a place of defeat.

"Nothing really. I mean, they're fine, you just don't meet girls who are, like, cool and driven."

"I'm sure they're on there."

"Maybe."

"C'mon, I'm sure you have ten hot girls in your phone from Tinder. I'm sure they're cool enough."

"Not really."

"Maybe you're not giving them a chance."

"You could be right. Sorry if I'm being too forward, I just don't always get to talk to, like, cool girls who are pretty and driven."

Chloe laughs. "Okay." She isn't sure if she wants the conversation to continue.

"Can I have your number?"

"I need to go back inside."

"That's fine. We can go back. Just give me your number first."

"I can't."

"Why?"

"I just can't man."

"It's just your number." Alex laughs, "You can give it to me and then, like, immediately block me. I'll never know!"

Chloe laughs.

"I'm not joking. Would you please just let me have your number? I don't love begging, but I guess that's what I am doing."

"How old are you?" Chloe isn't sure why she is asking the question—to give her space to deal with the unspoken content of their interaction, suddenly so naked, so spoken? Or is she curious to know where Alex sits on the timeline between her age and Sillyboi's? She should mention she has a boyfriend. *I have a boyfriend*, she could easily say. It's the truth.

"Twenty-three." Alex says.

"I thought you were older."

"Yeah. People do."

"I should get back."

"Cool. Yeah. Just give me your number first." Alex has his phone in his hands. Chloe takes his phone without thinking and inputs her number.

"I just called myself."

"Cool."

Alex smiles.

"Now you have it."

Chloe hands him his phone and walks back into the building.

•

The boys are saying goodbye and Chloe, still without a text from Sillyboi, entertains the mental image—with its corresponding olfactory hallucination—of Sillyboi on the subway; his cock reeking of Celeste. Chloe stares at her phone humiliated. Her phone vibrates. It's Sillyboi.

Wyd baby? I just realized it is pretty late

But, before she can lift a thumb to reply, exactly on cue, in one of those extraordinary moments in which it appears a heavenly operator does in fact control the cosmos —working his joystick with a conniving sense of humor— Chloe's phone vibrates with a text from Alex.

ELEVEN

Chloe steps on the subway platform headed in the opposite direction of Sillyboi. So far, there is no resistance between Chloe and transgression. Her lie was simple and plausible, and it began with a bit of truth: Chloe's best friend Simone has just returned from a backpacking trip in India and Sillyboi is aware of this fact. Simone is having trouble readjusting, Chloe lied, back to being a hostess at a West Village bar populated by frat boys; back to her closet-sized bedroom and the bathroom she shares with four other roommates; back to ordinary misery and temporary happiness, both of which feel boring and oppressive after the euphoric drama of travel. Valiantly, Chloe has offered herself as a "familiar body" to ease her best friend's transition from Far East bliss™ to American hastiness and corruption. This was Chloe's alibi and it was neither hard to invent nor difficult for Sillyboi to believe.

Above ground, Chloe inputs the address into Google maps and follows the thin blue line to an apartment in Chinatown. Chloe remembers Sillyboi's trip to SXSW. The entire time he was there they were communicating—they had just started dating and their texting was electric—Sillyboi was sending constant updates and telling her he loved her often. "Exhausted. Screening went great! Going to sleep early. I love you." Sleep early? *Could that have been when he fucked his whore? Or was it during the day in the bathroom of some disgusting Austin bar?* But wait, is Chloe's memory correct? Were they even admitting they loved each other then? Chloe wants to believe they were not, and that Sillyboi's affair happened before the debut of that momentous formulation. She wants to believe they had not yet fallen in love, as if that would absolve him and she could go home.

Chloe is standing face to face with a panel of buzzers. She locates the apartment number from their text history on a long rectangular jaundiced paper legend, under glass, framed in metal, and adjacent to the surname "Chen," either a roommate or previous tenant, and presses the button hard. The front door unlocks with a piercing vibration and a sound that is somehow native to the island of Manhattan where the buildings are not only older and taller, but louder.

Alex greets her at his door with a mumbled word and leads her into a long and narrow apartment eerily similar to her own. Two small doors on either end of the floor plan lead to minuscule bedrooms, she suspects, cubicles where one retires wasted or with the evening's fresh catch, also wasted, to thrust into for a moment or two and pause brutal consciousness. In the center of the apartment, a kitchen overflows with empty bottles and dirty dishes. Adjacent to the kitchen is a living area completely dominated by an early-aught's projection television and oversized coffee colored leather couch. Two roomates sit on the couch playing Xbox. Alex approaches the guys. Chloe lingers behind and wonders if she should turn and flee, profoundly terrified at the prospect of having to interact with roommates. What if she knows them? That would be a tragedy. On television, American soldiers wearing night vision goggles fire automatic rifles at an invading North Korean army in Seoul, and Alex turns around to ask her the lamest possible question.

"You ever play Call of Duty?"

"No."

Alex reaches over the gamers, eyes fixed on war, to grab a bag of weed and rolling papers.

"Do you have anything to drink?" Chloe asks.

Chloe follows Alex through one of the small doors and into a bedroom too small for the massive air conditioning unit blocking the room's only window. *Sillyboi would never allow this,* Chloe thinks, *a view of any kind is too precious to him.* Alex's room is disgusting: clothing pushed up against the walls, forgotten containers of food, empty bottles and cans, stacks of Con-Ed bills and Bank of America statements; and the smell, so much like the body of an unfamiliar man that even before an article of clothing is removed, Chloe feels she has already cheated. The odorant molecules containing Alex's scent penetrate her nostrils. Chloe waits for him to apologize for the chaos. He does not. Instead, he gathers what appear to be three pairs of sweatpants on the bed, and tosses them into a corner where jeans hang on top of a skateboard.

"You want something to drink, right?"

Chloe nods.

"Tequila or beer? I'm out of mixers though."

"Tequila's fine."

"No ice either, but it's cold."

If I get murdered, Chloe thinks, *Sillyboi will call Simone sometime tomorrow and discover I lied.* The thought of being murdered a cheating liar is not far off from Chloe's ultimate fantasy: to die tragically young and hot with loved ones tortured by conflicting feelings.

Chloe realizes with nostalgia that her fear of being murdered at the hands of a strange—or semi-strange—man has substantially decreased since moving in with Sillyboi. The fear of being murdered was among her most reliable companions during the period of promiscuity that preceded her relationship, moving freely from the bedroom of one potential murderer to another. Chloe is glad she is soft and weak and is not jealous of men for the handful of biological advantages that disconnect them from life's sweet precarity. ("Precarity" is a word my word-processing software was not designed to recognize. I just "added" "precarity" to my copy of Microsoft Word's internal dictionary and I can't help but wonder, is this resistance?)

Alex hands her a plastic cup filled to the brim with tequila and places his body carefully next to hers. The moment of transgression is fast approaching.

"Do you skate?" Chloe asks to break the silence.

"Ah, yeah, sort of," he says. "I manage professional skaters. So, I'm good by normal standards, but not by mine."

"I'm sure you're pretty good."

Chloe hears herself continue a light and flirtatious conversation with Alex as an image of Sillyboi, eyes closed and asleep, uploads to her consciousness. A cursor appears to click it away. It takes three unsuccessful clicks before the invading image is gone and Chloe hears herself agreeing that Bronze is cooler and arguably more relevant than Supreme, hoping the conversation will end so they can begin fucking. Alex keeps talking and Chloe is suddenly overcome by an outlandishly upbeat unhappiness. Sex is the only way out of this terrible feeling. Chloe presses her toes into the soles of her Docs. *This is not happening*, she says to herself in a calm direct tone like an actress playing a teacher in a movie with a message. *This is not happening*, she says again and again as the phrase becomes an illegible drumbeat, more soothing without meaning.

Alex stops talking and stares at her with a pained expression. His mouth opens and his face moves quickly toward hers. His tongue is wider and softer in her mouth than Sillyboi's and together their mouths produce more liquid than Chloe is accustomed to, his meaty lips more in proportion with her own, his breath rancid with alcohol, anxiety, and bad diet. Chloe is wet with disgust, wetter than with Sillyboi whose mouth is dry and breath is sweet.

It's as bad as you could possibly imagine, she nearly says out loud to Sillyboi who she imagines crouched next to the mini fridge, frozen in horror, fingernails tearing his scalp.

She helps Alex remove her wide black cargo pants so he can lick the area just above her underwear elastic. *This is so corny*, Chloe thinks watching Alex lick her stomach. And yet, isn't this one of the few arenas where corny reliably works: at children's parties, in the bedroom, etc.?

Chloe makes a sound and says a word as Alex takes the whole of her clitoris into his mouth and sucks it like a penis, his tongue stroking the entire organ with each suck. *This man has eaten a lot of snatch,* Chloe thinks, amused as "snatch" returns to her vocabulary after so long an absence. Sillyboi's rage is still in the room, now owned by her, it intensifies her pleasure. Chloe shudders, feeling closer than ever to Sillyboi. It only took twenty years to discover how the clit grows colossal with mischief. *Finally, I understand,* she thinks, *the best sex cucks.*

Chloe cums and is eager to take Alex in her mouth. His cock is thicker than Sillyboi's, miraculously clean, and smells slightly of mentholated soap. Chloe looks up at him, mouth full, and he regards her as one might an angel glimpsed from just outside the gilded gates of heaven.

"God, you're so fucking cute. Fuck, you're fucking so pretty," he says as she sucks him. *It is so like a man,* Chloe thinks, *to become affectionate precisely in the moment when I am least likely to respond.* Nonetheless, a primitive joy spreads through her body to hear her looks and charm confirmed as ropes of saliva fall from her mouth. This, she is certain, Sillyboi would hate the most: staring at each other, in wonder, as he pushes deeper down her throat.

"Do you want me to cum in your mouth?"

She hesitates, confused.

"Do you have a condom?" she asks.

"Why?" he asks.

She hesitates again, even more confused.

"I want to fuck," she says.

Alex turns her over and thinking is replaced by pleasure; by not seeing his face; by not knowing his mother; by not caring if she fed him with breast or with bottle; by not understanding his vanity; by having never seen him weep; by never imagining what their kids would look like; by not caring if they were cute or repulsive; by never picturing him old; by never hoping to know him then; by knowing nothing but this feeling. Chloe is euphoric with ignorance. He finishes quickly and she is flattered.

"Are you on birth control?"

Chloe nods.

"That was my last condom."

The second time they do not use a condom. Once finished, Chloe is still preoccupied with identifying which part of the evening Sillyboi would hate the most. Would it be how Alex held either side of her face as he climaxed? Would it be his semen, now in her cervix, fighting to the death with her IUD? Would it be his aggression? Would it be how she cried "daddy?" Or would it be how all of the expressions and sounds she made were likely identical to those she makes at home with him? No, none of this is damaging enough. What should boil his fury to the point of psychosis would be to observe them now: her body wrapped around his, the room silent but for their breath in rhythm.

He stirs to twenty five percent awake, finds her forehead, and kisses it.

Their cosplay of love approaches the real.

(Yes, I also added, "cosplay.")

TWELVE

Outside Alex's apartment, she walks briskly up Ludlow toward the M train on Delancey and Essex. *Was Alex's hair blonde or black? Did his cock actually taste like soap?* Chloe considers getting a blood test but decides against it, as the visit would produce—even on one server in a sad blockhouse surrounded by prairie where City MD archives their paperwork—a record of the encounter she is desperate to forget.

On the M train in Bushwick, Chloe sees into many small apartments and imagines couples living lives of pure romance as Alex becomes unforgettable. Her disassociation last night, which felt so delicious and complete, now sober and surrounded by commuters, is experienced for what it was: naïve delusion. And their conversation, which in the moment of its transmission, she believed she had succeeded in blocking from her memory, comes back to her in high definition. He was so interested in her! He craved her details: at what age she began to draw; when and why she got her first tattoo; how she practices; how many days a week; what she expects from the future? It was as if he came preprogrammed with all the qualities that would make her most susceptible. And, the sex, forgettable on the street running from his front door, is remembered on the train as fantasy-grade, generation-defining, trope-creating, earth-shattering. His intense interest, the perfect inverse of the insentient pounding and indifference of her inert partnership with Sillyboi. Should she run back to him? Should she call in sick and become his? She remembers a charming moment, in which, shy and eager for her approval, he showed her a skate video he produced. It was entertaining! "Very well done," she said, and was telling the truth! He has potential! Is this love? Why not love him who approached her by the dumpsters with his charming and intentional forgetting of his last cigarette? A story already awash with indefensible nostalgia for their kids! An antique guy they just don't make anymore! Approaching her by the dumpsters was not some brutish gesture of male entitlement; from what blog did she download that opinion? It was romantic! It was charming! It was fate! There is so much to learn about this Alex who looks like a prince and fucks like a king! *Oh, this is as bad as Sillyboi could possibly imagine*—the thought (now a personal meme) comes back to her—and all her fears are confirmed. Sillyboi and Celeste need not to have fucked to be plotting elopement. A decent conversation is all it takes! And, not only Celeste, but also every single girl he has worked with, passed on the street, or seen on his feed! They are all competition and Chloe has lost the will to fight! She must return to Alex! Alex, the wise; Alex, the faithful; Alex, in whose presence she was confident and loquacious; Alex, who saved her from neurotic apologizing; Alex, who would save her from all of life's enraging inequities; their perfect partnership commencing in his shoebox room, strewn with detritus. Chloe, the only ray of light capable of bending past his enormous, impractical, perfectly adorable, air-conditioning unit.

Chloe opens Instagram and scrolls. Her feed is dominated by black-work neo-traditional and traditional tattoos. They are soothing. *This is my destiny,* she thinks, *bold tattooing, black work with a limited color palette.* Instagram and her ambition are the distraction she needs. Her mind is made up. She will leave Sillyboi tomorrow to be with Alex if tonight concludes in an argument, bad sex, or loud breathing.

Chloe enters the shop through the back door to delay the ordeal of opening the front gate and drawing any unwanted attention to her presence, hours before she would normally arrive to do the morning chores—sweeping, mopping, emptying trash cans, putting fresh paper towels at each station—preparing the business for feast or famine. Chloe lies on the leather sofa, sets an alarm for noon, and sleeps.

A call wakes her fifteen minutes before noon and the pressure in her heart is so intense, a sob nearly replaces a proper greeting.

"Hi baby." Sillyboi's voice is heavy with sleep. "Are you still at Simone's?"

"Hi, no, I just got to the shop."

"Oh right."

"Did you just wake up?" She says, and rises from the

sofa, skin sticking to leather.

"Yeah."

"Aw. I bet you look cute."

"I bet you look cute."

"Stop. I don't." She says, spotting her reflection in the window.

"No?"

"Maybe. I don't know."

"I missed you last night sweetheart," he says, and, upon hearing this simple statement, Chloe is visited by a feeling of regret so powerful it may linger in her body for the rest of her life; thick clumps of regret present in her ashes after cremation. This is the feeling she wished upon Sillyboi: shame—debilitating, destabilizing shame—with the power to derail a body from its frantic search for pleasure.

"You missed me?"

"So much, sweet baby."

"Aw. I could cry."

"Oh baby. You're the cutest little baby."

"You're the cutest little baby."

Sillyboi makes a vague sound with his throat and Chloe senses he is distracted. She unconsciously tries a familiar tactic.

"Ugh, I'm so horny right now, baby," she says.

"We'll fuck when you get home."

"I can't wait that long."

"You'll have to wait, baby, unless you want me to come fuck you in one of those disgusting bathrooms where you work."

Chloe laughs.

"Will you send me a picture of that big cock? I am literally dying for it."

"Right now?"

"Yeah."

"Okay."

Three minutes later, a photo of Sillyboi's perfectly average cock is delivered into Chloe's phone.

She texts:

I'm wet
Good
Seriously Silly I'm gonna be wet all day thinking about us fucking later
Me too

•

A young woman with ice-blue hair and a piercing through her medial cleft is standing at the front desk. Chloe musters professional composure. It's easier to locate than expected, still hung over from adultery. The young woman is April. She saw Chloe's flash on Instagram and wants to get one of her pieces: a Sailor Jerry-esq pinup with stripper accouterment. (Ring, ring, who's there, hello, it's the money.)

April wants the tattoo on her ankle.

The timing of April, Chloe's first official customer, neither a walk-in nor a friend offering their skin as practice canvas, is odd. Shouldn't today's work be repaying karmic debt? Shouldn't her mood be sullen and reflective? Why is life offering a reward? April, arriving in the dead of winter, a total stranger who could have selected any tattooer in New York City, and she yet chose Chloe. A milestone! A gift! The holiest scratch-off ticket won!

Chloe suppresses neurotic apologies. *I suck at this, my tattoos don't heal well, I'm still just an apprentice.* Chloe hands April a consent form. Chloe convenes with Otis who gives his consent with a nod. Chloe positions April on a long massage table. Chloe stencils the stripper on her ankle. Chloe connects her machine to a power supply. Chloe proceeds with a calm so profound that the events in her life, confusing and haphazard disappointments and setbacks, appear perfectly in sequence, each roadblock revealed to be a secret bridge to bring this moment into being. Chloe's machine springs to life with its beautiful, angry, hypnotic buzz.

•

That night, Sillyboi returns to their apartment in an uncharacteristically pleasant mood.

"Great day at the office!" He exclaims with the inflection of a sitcom husband. Chloe, playing the role of "wife," playfully tackles him to the hardwood floor.

"I had a breakthrough with my script, I think! Finally, finally, finally!" Sillyboi sings—hip bruised—as Chloe laughs and her body fills with a horrifying quantity of love.

"Let's hit the bong!" She says and jumps to her feet.

Rushing to fetch it, Chloe catches a whiff of her own scent, and remembers her last shower was yesterday morning, before work. Before Alex.

"Wait, will you pack it baby?"

Chloe slams the bathroom door, undresses, and inhales her clothing, overcome by the smell of sex. Everything reeks of Alex, whose face re-enters her brain like a seizure. She conceals the offensive articles at the bottom of an already full laundry basket and jumps into the shower so hot she suffers the eerie lag of suspense, the neurological drop, as a bolt of agony travels up her spinal cord and into the primitive section of her brain. Sillyboi enters the bathroom, holding the bong over his head like a trophy awarded to the sweetest boyfriend in Bushwick.

"Don't come in!" Chloe shouts as Sillyboi sits down heavily on the flimsy toilet seat. The outburst nearly incriminates her. What reason would she have to eject him other than to shield his eyes from the spectacle of her body, bruised, and covered in blistering sores, reeking with the treacherous stink of duplicity. "I am discovered," she nearly moans at the volume of the Greeks, "guilty, I am guilty, guilty!"

"What was that?" Sillyboi asks, smiling and stoned.

Tears well into the corners of her eyes.

"I burned myself!"

"Aw, I'm sorry, sweet baby."

Through the translucent shower curtain, Sillyboi stares at her, opens his mouth, and lolls his tongue forward to produce an obscene arpeggio of gagging noises and smoke.

Chloe pretends to be amused. Sillyboi, emboldened, merrily gulps down more smoke before opening the shower curtain to offer her a hit.

"Silly! Don't! It'll get wet!"

"Lean your head out of the stream!" Sillyboi lights the

bong just outside the shower's spray. Chloe exhales a cloud into the humidity of the shower.

"Don't you think there's something, like, hypermodern about the whole mouth-open-tongue-out thing?"

"I don't know what you're talking about, Silly."

"What I just did!" Sillyboi takes another hit. "With my mouth open and my tongue out. That's, like, a...you know what I'm talking about." Sillyboi sounds like a disgruntled prophet festering with ignored prophecies "That's a thing. That's, like, a modern gesture."

"Is it?"

"Oh, come on Chloe, it is. It absolutely is. Girls do it on Instagram to look hot or something. Guys too, I guess. People do it to try and look hot, but, like, undercut that impulse or whatever. It's, like, look at me, I'm hot, but I'm also being ironic about it. Or underlining it actually. People always think things are ironic but that's not true, people are actually really sincere these days, but anyway, it's stupid, it's like a thing you do when you wanna look hot, it's, like, objectively hot."

"I guess."

"But the point is, it's new. People didn't make that face in the eighties or nineties, and they definitely didn't do it in the fifties! And, like, it does totally make sense culture would, like, give birth to something like this mouth open, tongue out thing now." Sillyboi inhales deeply, high on weed and the belief he has finally discovered an important and unique worldview.

"Do you know what it is, actually?" Sillyboi continues, "That face? It's, like, the essence of late capitalism reduced to a facial expression. Does that make sense? It's the body defining itself as an orifice for consumption. Like, we're transforming the face into nothing holier than a hole for pleasure and consumption without consequence! We have cut ourselves off from higher impulses! Fucking, mouth open tongue out! We are jokes! It really is the perfect invention for the day! With your mouth open, you can't… the will to fight is destroyed! Has anyone ever gone into battle with their mouth open and their tongue out like that? It's not possible. Nothing radical is possible, revolution is not possible as long as that hideous juvenile expression defines us!" Chloe is silent for a long moment before speaking.

"I think you're missing the point Sillyboi."

"Oh really? Am I? Enlighten me then, on the point I'm missing, dearest Chloe."

"It's not serious."

"But, that's…! No! I reject that! It's ridiculous how often, I mean, do we really want that to be our jingle? Our legitimizing jingle? 'It's not serious?' Okay, why not write a little tune and make that into an ad or something! 'It's not serious.' Well, guess what, life is serious regardless of how intensely we seek to find evidence that it's not!"

"Silly…"

"I get that people want to look sexy online and be obscene and attract the opposite sex, or whatever. And, it's no big deal, sure, but that's just, like, right in the center of the point I am trying to make. Why? Why is it no big deal to present your face in a photo that will live forever on the Internet as a basic fucking orifice to get fucked? Like here's my open hole world, here it is! But, God forbid, God forbid you ever do anything to actually question my behavior, or offend me, or question my perfect fucking politics! Then may God have mercy on your disgusting problematic soul, for I shall call you out! Publicly! On the Internet! I will scream about you in the modern coliseum! The stadium packed with everyone you've ever met! Everyone in the world! And that, my friend is murder! That's the exact same thing as murder!"

"Sillyboi! Stop!"

"What?"

"Jesus Christ! You sound paranoid. No one's going to call you out!" Chloe suddenly looks worried. "Are they?"

"No!" Sillyboi laughs. "I'm going to write a think piece. On Open Mouths. That's the title. Of my think piece. Perfectly pampered whiteface and blackface performers of identity. Without substance. Without anything really other than constant projection of opinions! Of ideology de jour! Without anything! Without real analysis! It's so stupid. It's the worst nightmare. A society of bullshit consumers, of things and ideas and people and activism! Today activism is a fucking outfit! Hash-tag your entire belief system that no one really understands!"

Sillyboi glares at her with quiet rage. "And, I know you think this is stupid. Or trite. Or mean, or privileged, or white, or misogynistic, or something, but actually, I wish what I'm saying was triter! It's not trite enough! My hope, my sincere hope for humanity is that we live to see a day when the shit I'm saying actually does sound stupid and old. Like, a thing of the past. Everyone we know is benefiting from the structures they claim to be oppressed by unless they're actually fucking poor and victimized, which not a single person we know is, sorry. So, I don't want to hear shit from them. Online or off. And, one last thing, before I shut up, I know each generation had their, like, gestural tropes, or whatever, like throwing up the peace sign, but the mouth open, tongue out thing, or when a person sticks their finger in there? The, like, sexy, in quotes, face we show to the world, that is actually a mask we use to distract people, and especially ourselves, from the gruesome fact that while we post our cute fucking cool nonsense bullshit into the void, we are literally adding currency to the fascists who actually run shit! The oligarchs who would liquefy every single mouth open tongue out in concentration camps the second shit actually started to hit the fan! Or maybe they would all just fly to mars on the handful of mars planes and leave us to burn up and die!"

"Sillyboi!"

"What?"

"Jesus!"

"You know I'm right!"

"You sound crazy. Or, like, alt-right, or something. It's weird."

"Alt-right? L.M.A.O. I am so far left, I'm left out. Also, I'm too psychoanalyzed to be alt-right."

"Oh my god."

"What? I have strong opinions. That's a good thing."

"Can you stop now? I thought we were going to have a nice night."

Sillyboi starts laughing.

"What?"

"I'll make sure not to send you the link."

"What?"

"To my think piece. When it's published."

"I thought you had a good day. You were supposed to be in a good mood, but you're just being mean."

"Mean?"

"Yes!"

"This is my real personality, Chloe. Maybe you don't like my real personality."

"I hate when you say that."

"I'm happy. I never said I wasn't happy."

"What?"

"Whatever."

"What are you saying?"

"Nothing."

Sillyboi fiddles with the bong. Chloe turns off the shower and reaches for a towel.

"How was your day?" he asks feebly.

"Um, good?"

"That's all?"

Truth would be the perfect antidote, Chloe thinks, *to Sillyboi's annoying monologue*. But she doesn't want the conversation to end; the longer he spews his venom, the less likely she is to incriminate herself.

"So, nothing happened at the shop?" Sillyboi says.

"No. Not really. Kind of a boring day. Everyone was late, as usual. I managed to do a little drawing, but nothing I'm proud of."

"I'm sure it was good."

This will be my lie, Chloe thinks, *I'll even wait a few days to post April's tattoo.* Her secret triumph subsumes her disloyalty, and she steps out of the shower.

"It really wasn't good."

"Well. I'm sorry."

"It's not your fault."

Sillyboi moves his knees to make room for Chloe. She brushes her hair in front of the mirror. Chloe glances at him, still sitting on the toilet seat, knees jammed into the wall, and notices his certitude has morphed, stoop shouldered, to contrition.

"I didn't really mean what I said."

"What?"

"The thing about my real personality. That's so dumb. That's annoying. I'm annoying sometimes."

Chloe braids her hair.

"Baby?" Sillyboi says.

"I know you're annoying."

"I don't give a shit about anything I just said. Fuck. I gotta stop doing that."

"What?"

"Saying things I don't agree with. I feel like I'm always doing it. It's really stupid."

Chloe puts down the brush and looks at him intensely. "Are you really always saying things you disagree with? Because, if that's true, it really worries me."

"No! No! I get how that sounds. No, I'm just stoned. I'm philosophizing and I'm stoned and I sound like an idiot. Please don't listen to me. My ideas are dumb. I say things to sound smart and I usually just wind up sounding pretentious and retarded."

"You're not retarded, you're just high."

"Thank you."

"Let me roll you a joint. That bong gets you too high."

Chloe taps the grinder three times on her desk to expel the last pieces of weed from its lime green plastic teeth. Sillyboi slides over to her, places his hand on the back of her neck, and asks if she is feeling any better. Calmly, Chloe responds in the affirmative as she crosses her toes to cancel the lie.

Sillyboi drops to the floor and buries his face in her lap.

"Silly?"

He rotates his head to look up at her.

"I can't roll this with your face there."

Sillyboi stands and picks up a piece of flash from her desk: a single eye with a long tear dripping from the duct framed by an eyebrow the same shape Chloe draws on her own face every morning.

"I would get this." he says.

"Take it." She says, carefully moving a mound of weed into the rolling paper.

"As a tattoo, I mean. I could see myself getting this as a tattoo."

Chloe looks up at him.

"What are you talking about?"

"Can you do this on me?"

"No," she says, unhappiness expanding fast, "stop."

"What do you mean, no?"

"Sillyboi." It takes every ounce of her will to remain calm. "You just finished explaining how you always say things you don't actually mean. So, how am I supposed to respond to you wanting a tattoo from me now? It's unfair." She licks the joint closed. "I want it too much."

"Oh baby. No! I really love this! I remember when you posted it. I thought it was awesome!" Sillyboi holds the design to the lamp light.

"Don't!" Chloe says, angry.

"What do you mean?"

"Don't do this right now."

"Baby," Sillyboi kneels and holds her face. His pulse hammers through the center of his palms, "I need a tattoo from you," he says with sonnet intensity simulating the platonic ideal of "the lover." "How could I not have one from you? Oh, I love you so much my sweet little sweetheart. My baby. My sweetest little baby. How could I let all these idiots walk around Bushwick with tattoos from you and not have one myself? Please. Will you do it for me?"

If only he weren't so convincing, she would run back to Alex who returns to her now. But just before she slaps Silly and runs from their apartment, euphoric and emancipated, Chloe realizes this too—this tattoo—is another desire too precious to be muttered. This, she has wanted since first seeing Sillyboi naked, blank, and white like paper on her bed. This permanence will solve them.

"What do you mean, need?" she asks.

"Now that I have one tattoo. I need another from you. A Chloe tattoo."

Her brand on her boy! Her sweet little cattle! She shrieks, melts into his body, and returns to the womb.

"Where should it go?" she asks from the womb.

"It can't be my arms." His voice sounds gorgeous from inside the womb. Chloe is born. She takes a step back and studies him.

"Shh! I know."

She's Michelangelo looking at stone.

"Take off your sock," she commands, and places the eye on the top of his foot.

"Here!"

Sillyboi looks down, "oh," he says.

"What?"

He is silent.

"What?"

"That's…yeah."

"You don't like it?"

"No. No!" He has tears in his eyes, "it's perfect."

THIRTEEN

Chloe sits in Super Happy. Otis texts, watching the clock and waiting for a reasonable time to leave early, while Sean tattoos an Art Nouveau cat on a goth girl's wrist. Chloe texts Sillyboi to see if he's changed his mind about the eye tattoo. He has not. Her one good machine broken, Chloe sneaks one of Otis's machines from his drawer and stuffs it alongside other supplies she is too poor to buy (ink, inkwells, clip-chord, stencil-paper, power-supply) into her backpack.

Walking home, the gear is a time machine, flashing her into the future, allowing her to be present at Sillyboi's funeral. She smiles at the idea: her eye on his body, surveilling his life, shedding a single tear as he decomposes. The sidewalk is dusty with synthetic salt. Chloe pulls her coat together and shivers in the cold.

Using a cobalt blue Bic single-use razor, Chloe strokes away a small patch of hair from the top of Sillyboi's foot, to transfer the stencil onto a clean surface. Will the hair there thicken with age and obscure her vision?

"Are you ready, kid?" she asks.

He nods. Of all the tattoos not to fuck up, this is the one. Chloe will accept nothing but perfection, not a single blown out line, or incomplete stroke. Become the machine is her mantra.

"This is supposed to be a really painful spot." She is tattooing him now, pressing apart the skin, making it taut, stroking the machine as gently as watercolor.

"Yeah it hurts."

"Sorry."

"I actually like the feeling."

"It won't take much longer."

"I don't want it to end."

Chloe knows she feels pain more intensely than other people, and each time she submits herself to a tattooer's needle, it's a feat aided by two, three, or even four Vicodin: a flirtation with an old addiction and a concession to a new one. "Those who are most sensitive, should administer pain to others," she's heard, and so, with each addition to her tattoo collection, she becomes better equipped for her desired role: artist as giver and receiver of pain. Sillyboi, whose feelings are so easily bruised, sits for the needle as if in a coma.

Twenty minutes later, it's finished. The room is silent. Chloe douses Sillyboi's foot with disinfectant and wipes away the blood and excess ink with a paper towel. Chloe cleans the tattoo a second time and Sillyboi winces.

"Okay, that really hurt."

Chloe looks down and sees, wiped clean on hairless skin, her first tattoo without a mistake. Not one blow-out. It is perfect. This is how she owns him.

They dance and kiss. They hold each other and jump up and down as Nicole blasts Iggy Azalea and Drake. They laugh and laugh for thirty-five minutes and even stock away some surplus hilarity, enough to get them through whatever tragedies lie ahead.

•

Sillyboi sits in a cafe, dense with freelancers, desperately trying to finish the screenplay that will make him a celebrity. His new tattoo healing, stinging, and wrapped in Saran. On the toilet this morning, confronting for the first time, without Chloe, his modified foot, Sillyboi was gripped by regret.

My foot is crying. It will always be crying. What does this mean? Is this depression? He had to find an alternate reading; or, at the very least settle for a light non-reading. A tattoo is just fashion! Ubiquitous decoration! No, that's not it. Maybe a tattoo is a talisman to ward off depression? If the foot is in anguish, can the heart now be open and free? Yes, that's it! Oh, praise the secular God without dogma who resembles the handful of celebrity monks who've sold Sillyboi books! His first tattoo redefined him, inaugurated a new era with a new spelling for a new man, confronting life with "I" out front, always the subject taking action with style. Now, his second tattoo cures him! All he needed was figurative "sadness," placed low on the body to conduct torment from the psyche to the ground, like a lightning rod, and inject all the roaches with large frequent doses of yid neurosis! The tattoo is a ticket to permanent happiness! No, none of this. His tattoos are just chivalry, dumb shit, you do once or twice, to impress your girlfriend. Sillyboi settles on this interpretation and opens Final Draft, filled with frustration, to finish his great-unfinished work: *Launching Pad*.

Sillyboi retitles the document *Launching Pad* Version 3.0 to begin a new idea. The year is 1999. Fade in on Riverdale Country School, a private prep school in the wealthiest section of the Bronx, attended by Manhattan's most privileged progeny. The film focuses on the social dynamics of a clique of seventh grade boys considered "popular" given their physical status as top athletes and their emotional status as social terrorists. Riverdale is eighty percent white and ninety percent affluent. After the sixth grade, students move from the River Campus, which begins in kindergarten, to the Hill Campus where they spend their middle school years adjusting to the new environment. Also, in seventh grade, class size increases with an influx of students from private elementary schools that do not have a corresponding middle school, as well as from organizations like Prep For Prep, which select intellectually gifted minority students from disadvantaged backgrounds and place them, on full scholarship, in schools like Riverdale, paving their way to prestigious universities so they may be qualified, as adults, for positions in society that maintain the inequities of the status quo and oppress the disadvantaged, like their parents and former peers.

The film begins with one of the new seventh graders, Evan Ambrosio, arriving into the popular clique of boys to become the protagonist of *Launching Pad* Version 3.0 retitled, in a masterstroke of genius, *Seventh Grade*.

Evan arrives at Riverdale in the privileged position of already being a good acquaintance of the de facto ringleader of the jock bullies: Asher Perlman, a pale, curly haired **[REDACTED]** with dark freckles, buckteeth, and suspiciously sloped button nose. Evan and Asher met at Wildwood camp where Evan was "the best motherfucking Lacrosse player since Hairy Harry Man-Child Bergman." Evan, "definitely not a **[REDACTED]** scored hat-tricks in three games against Deerkill." Ambrosio is automatically friends with the clique who do not know he is a quarter Black, his mother and maternal grandparents being mixed race. Evan, olive skin, looks like his father, who is Italian. The bullies, however, assume he is Jewish like them.

Between drop off and first period, students gather in the cafeteria to buy egg-and-cheese sandwiches and expel adolescent anger in the form of conversation and comedy.

Asher escorts Evan to a table where a group of boys are discussing who will be present in the Hamptons this weekend and which house will serve as the venue for their group sleepover/viewing party of *Junior College Hardcore Schoolgirls 4* by Max Hardcore. Sam Solomon, a tall towhead with blue eyes and bowl-cut, discovered the VHS along with many others in his uncle's attic den in Tahoe. Max Hardcore, according to Solomon, is an energetic redneck who appears in and produces his own pornography where girls are sodomized and mouth-fucked with no cut between the actions. Mr. Hardcore was the man who discovered how to piss through a boner and into a lady's mouth. *Junior College Hardcore Schoolgirls 4*, released that August, is the perfect tool to discover who among them can cum real cum and who has been lying for all of sixth grade.

Evan, who can't cum and doesn't want to claim he can, keeps his mouth shut as Gideon Goldstein—a thirteen-year-old who looks ten—argues in favor of his "big wet loads," when Noa Bretholtz, a sophomore famous for blowing seniors in the faculty bathroom, saunters into the cafeteria covered in baby blue Juicy Couture velour, her hooded jacket unzipped to reveal a yellow camisole.

Noa draws attention away from Goldstein, who prays his glacial puberty accelerates in the coming days before group masturbation, likely to take place in his parent's screening room in Southampton, where the boys will expect Goldstein to present a handful of fresh product without going first to the bathroom to pawn a puddle of conditioner off as the real McCoy.

INT. HIGH SCHOOL CAFETERIA - MORNING

                    SOLOMON
          (Interrupting the cum debate)
     Oh shit, look look, look! Here comes
     blowjob Noa with her tahs out!

Solomon gestures as if cupping his own pendulous breasts. Noa glances at the boys but pretends not to hear them.

                    SOLOMON
     Jesus Christ! Look at those things! You can
     see her nips! They're fucking dinner
     plates!

EVAN
(Trying hard to be alpha, shouts)
D.P's!

SOLOMON
Look at those tay's! Look at those tah's!
Look at those ti-tay-tahs!

PEARLMAN
Bet you guys didn't know I titty fucked
Noa. Bet I'm the only person here who's
titty fucked ever!

SOLOMON
Shut up Perlman! You didn't titty fuck Noa!
Stop being such a **[REDACTED]**.

PERLMAN
Why don't you stop your mom from having
cancer?

This quiets the group. Solomon looks upset. His
mother does, in fact, have breast cancer.

PERLMAN
It was at Barron Levy's brother's
graduation party on the Bowery last summer.
I bet you weren't invited. I titty fucked
Noa. I told her I was in the tenth grade at
Buckley and she believed me.

GOLDSTIEN
D'you cum?

PERLMAN

What do you mean, did I cum? You've clearly
never cum in your entire life, Goldstein! I
came on her nipples!

SOLOMON

Go fuck yourself Perlman! You show me your
cock every time we're in Connecticut! It's
not big enough to fit between Noa's tits!
And no fucking way she'd believe you're a
sophomore at Buckley! Those **[REDACTED]** are
all on steroids!

The conversation migrates from the veracity of
Perlman's titty fucking Noa to the Knicks, which players
should be traded, where, and for who, when Trevon Lewis, a
Black student from the junior class walks into the cafeteria
to sit at a table near pebbled-glass chicken-wire windows,
where a small group of students of color have segregated
themselves. Gabe Tishman, brown hair, freckles, and lime
green rubber bands in his braces, interrupts the conversation.

TISHMAN

Oh shit, guys! Guys! Shut up for a second.

PERLMAN

What?

TISHMAN

Here comes Everett. Quick, hide your stuff!

What more potent injection of steroid to transform Sillyboi from struggling actor to uncompromising auteur, than to expose the racism and misogyny of his high school peers? Sillyboi is intoxicated by the possibilities! 2015 is the perfect year to expose the privileged private school Jews of the early aughts for the classist bigots they were and likely still are!

Zoom in on Evan's forced smile as the conversation devolves even further into malice. "Trevon's going to the **[REDACTED]** table." "Good thing they keep them all there." "The **[REDACTED]** table!" Solomon sings like a demented Hammerstein, which is cue for the others to repeat the jingle. A verse in their manic nightmare chorus. "You know why they sit together, right, don't you? They're trying to figure out how to steal our stuff!" "How do they afford to go here, again? Like, I don't get it. Aren't they poor?" "It's the scholarship table, moron!" Scholarship!!" Goldstein sings. Ever wonder why tuition is so high?" "Why?" We're paying for the table!" Perlman and others sing. "The table!" "The table!" Goldstein, Tishman, and more sing back. "Is that true?" "Of course, it's true, **[REDACTED]**! My dad's on the board!" The boys all laugh. "You think they could get in here if they weren't Black?" "Or Mexican?" "Good thing we got Mexicans though. Gotta have someone to mow the lawn!" The boys laugh again. Evan's smile stretches to the breaking point. Perspiration drips from Sillyboi's armpits, down his side, and into the waistline of his long underwear. (Is Sillyboi ready for the repercussions of his impulses? Will he survive—a white man drinking the dregs of the drink that was the era of the white man—writing the worst that can be written and calling it Art?) Sillyboi looks up from his laptop to a Black man sitting across from him wearing an oversized blazer, and layered, tattered, cable knit sweaters. *He knows,* Sillyboi thinks, *this guy knows I've been writing* **[REDACTED],** *writing it and re-writing it, for the past hour and a half.* Sillyboi feels the eyes of a woman, around his age, a copy of *I Love Dick* next to her laptop, covered in stickers, glance at his face, then away. *She knows too, as will my mother, as will every woman in America, I write characters who degrade, objectify, and verbally abuse women.*

Sillyboi will not survive. Finally, an idea that feels worthy of his time and effort! A screenplay that must be written! Sillyboi imagines the coffee shop is the court of public opinion and the freelancers, hunched over their laptops, doing their personal best to change or subvert culture, are the jurors.

"I am not racist! I am not sexist! Those are my characters, not me!" Sillyboi wails at the mob, gnashing their teeth, ready to pounce. Should he admit his characters and their hate are taken directly from his memory and that for the first time, he is using his own experience as material! Should he include this as evidence for the jury or save it for *Film Comment*? Isn't truth what audiences crave? Truth and Identity? Identity, plus emotion, plus craft, plus time, equals art, does it not? Is his Identity off-limits?

"You're capitalizing off the suffering of others! A woman in the back screams at the top of her lungs.

"Stop showing my people in disarray!" the barista adds and sprinkles cinnamon on a macchiato.

"But it's the truth! I witnessed this!" He says.

The freelancers erupt in a single voice of dissent, "No!"

Sillyboi collapses to the fetal position and takes the position he thinks they want, "It's all my fault! I am to blame! I am white! I am a man! I suck! I am trash! I am trash! I am nothing! Kill me! Just kill me!! Please kill me!!" The mob explodes in a chorus of jeers, throwing coffee cups, some of them full, at his laptop and face, driving him into the street, disgraced.

FOURTEEN

Sillyboi paces in front of his apartment as parishioners file out of the church next door with expressions rejuvenated by religion. A family climbs aboard a maroon passenger van with the church's logo painted on the side. Two elderly ladies sit on a bench built around the trunk of a frail tree. Sillyboi enters his building feeling ugly, stupid, and morally bankrupt.

Stoned, Sillyboi sits on the sofa scrolling through @celestescott focusing on a photo, two years old, of Celeste on the edge of what must be a rooftop pool, her foot perched on the pedestal of a white statue of Aphrodite, back arched, body taut under a black bikini. The photo, taken from a distance, is grainy—either disposable camera or filter—but Celeste's expression is unmistakable; mouth open, tongue out. A subtle mark of tension in her forehead as if caught in the moment leading up to orgasm. Sillyboi imagines a short scene in which she, making the same expression, masturbates on the carpet in front of him. The sound of Chloe's key turning the lock interrupts his reverie. Sillyboi buries his phone in the couch. Chloe jumps on him.

"I brought my tattoo stuff home again!" she says.

"Yeah?"

Chloe nods, smiling impishly.

"I want you to tattoo me tonight." Chloe tries to choke him with her tongue. Sillyboy flips her on her back and pins her arms above her head. He tries to bite her lips, but she uses her tongue as a shield.

"I want to bite them!" he says.

"Will you please tattoo me?" she replies.

"I don't know how."

"I'll teach you."

"I suck at drawing."

"I want words."

"They're going to suck. What words?"

"It doesn't matter how they look. You know what I want."

"I do?"

"You do."

Sillyboi can't guess.

"I don't know! Baby, tell me!"

"You know!"

"I really don't!"

She smiles. "Only the best!"

"What?"

"Only the best!"

"Only the best?"

"Only the best!"

•

The Origin of Only the Best!

ONLY THE BEST! has fallen out of fashion with Chloe and Sillyboi, but when the phrase was born, springing from Chloe's lips like Athena from the head of Zeus, it became so ubiquitous, it served as a substitute for all expressions. When language failed, "Only the Best!" was on the tongue to dive the speaker to ridiculous trenches or bounce them to balconies of sublimity.

To tell *The Origin of Only the Best!* I must go back before Chloe and Sillyboi, when Sillyboi was Sillyboy, and returned to the City from L.A., to move in with his parents, an anxious angry youth of twenty-six. Sillyboy left L.A. because he was not booking. The non-booking was surprising, given Sillyboy arrived in L.A. as one of the fresh new faces of network television. After rounds of auditions in cute little offices crammed with executives, Sillyboy landed the lead on *In Cell*, a CBS procedural centered on a celibate hacker recruited by the CIA to track down religious extremists plotting terror attacks. Critics instantly cried "Islamophobia!" "Another forgettable addition to the white savior canon." Entertainment Weekly gave the series a lukewarm review, but praised Sillyboy's "preternatural fluency with dull arcane dialogue." Sillyboy loved that line and considered making a personal website now that he could finally include a link to "press."

The beauty of starring in television, even canceled television, is it makes an actor momentarily wealthy and saleable enough to attract one of the best agents in town.

"Town" is a euphemism for L.A., which resembles a town like panna cotta resembles cum. At first, the relationship between Sillyboy and the best agent in town was strong. Sillyboy was reading A-list scripts and attending A-list auditions. But the face of *In Cell* was not booking. Sillyboy's fear as to why he was not booking was that, like most actors, he might also be delusional about the size of his talent. Delusion is hard to parse in oneself, especially when constantly practicing delusion, and delusion itself is the bedrock of your craft.

While Sillyboy was struggling to book, his girlfriend Ms. Slow Death was booking and booking and booking, riding a cresting wave of press for her first ever role as the star of Nicolas Winding Refn's *Girlboss*. Critics were unanimous: a star is born in Ms. Slow Death. Eric Kohn described her in *Indiewire* as "a talent who touches down once or twice in a century...a vessel: she is not merely acting, she is channeling the ancients...the camera doesn't adore her, it falls to its knees in worship." Ms. Slow Death privately denounced the review as objectifying; but still, it was re-posted with a long caption and loving emojis.

Sillyboy was eventually dropped by the best agent in town and discarded by Ms. Slow Death as he screamed, hit himself, and berated her for becoming a star. Ms. Slow Death gazed at Sillyboy who had fallen limp with envy. He had cheated, and in doing so, developed a taste for a new flavor of transgression. All was lost in Los Angeles. Sillyboy had to leave. Ivan was the only one sad to see him go. Everyone else was too busy thinking about pilot season.

Sillyboy arrived at his parent's apartment in Brooklyn

and onto the couch—where his mother's patients lie for psychoanalysis—feeling like the world's biggest loser. It didn't matter that his bank account was swollen from television or that he would find another agent, Sillyboy returned to the City emasculated by missed opportunities and possessed by fantasies of revenge. *I'll show them,* Sillyboy thought, *Ms. Slow Death, and those Hollywood bastards! I'll rise up and burn them with my intellect, talent, and the unique magical quality that inhabits everything about me!*

Doing his best to fall asleep on the couch, Sillyboy saw only one path toward the reclamation of his power: find a 19-year-old girl on the Internet to fuck.

So, with an erection staining his pants and morality dialed down to the lowest setting, Sillyboy set up a profile on *OkCupid*.

New to online dating, the first thing Sillyboy noticed, as he scrolled rows of available girls, was their ages displayed prominently next to their photo and username. Contained in this functional association was a revelation: this was the only tool available to a man nearing the twilight of his twenties for meeting and fucking barely legal girls.

Sillyboy's formative years were lived in a fantasy world created by "teen porn." Sillyboy was drawn to this pornography as the actresses in the videos resembled his high school peers: sitting cross-legged in hallways with low-slung jeans revealing ass cracks, whose juvenile confidence terrified him, who he had neither the poise nor audacity to approach.

Porn producers were eager to present the age of their actresses to the viewer and draw attention to the hard numerical value of the girl. The closer to legal rock bottom, the more valuable. Sillyboy's favorite videos included an interview before the fucking, in which the man behind the camera asks the girl questions to show her personality. (This kind of video often took the format of "humiliating audition," which Sillyboy found deeply relatable.) During the interview, Sillyboy believed he could sense if a girl was nervous, confident, or feigning confidence; or if she was intelligent, stupid, fearful, or on drugs. The girls responded to inane questions about their favorite sex positions or if they had boyfriends back home. Each question designed to titillate the viewer. All of it irrelevant to Sillyboy save one question: "How old are you?"

"How old are you sweetheart?"

"Nineteen," she would admit with world-weariness, at which point the producer would repeat the number for emphasis, as if the subject of his video were an endangered species of tree frog posing for the last time before extinction.

OkCupid allowed Sillyboy to limit the age range of his potential matches so the only girls served to his browser were teenagers. It felt similar to searching "real teenage amateur," "cute teen," or "freshman dorm room fuck party," on *Pornhub*. Sillyboy had never had sex with a teen, not even when he himself was a teen, and with his twenty-seventh birthday fast approaching, he believed he was entering the last era in which he could fuck an 18 or 19-year-old, while still within some morally acceptable boundary.

It wasn't too long into scrolling that he found her. Her profile described her as white and Asian. She listed her income as "over 10 million." Her "what I'm doing with my life" read "living the ice bucket challenge." Her "self-summary" read "every morning I wake up miserable because I am not the plug." She was cool. She was beautiful. She was 19.

wolfewolf: hello

Ten hours passed.

Inkdkitty: hii
wolfewolf: what's up?
Inkdkitty: not much just smoking and drawing
wolfewolf: cool. Sounds fun. What kind of stuff do you draw?
Inkdkitty: basically nothing. stuff for school.
wolfewolf: sounds fun. Where do you go?
Inkdkitty: nyu. lmao.
wolfewolf: you don't like it?
Inkdkitty: not really. wyd?
Sillyboy googled, "what does 'wyd' mean in a text?"
wolfewolf: about to go to the gym get swol. grrrr.

Sillyboy immediately regretted the "grrrr." In an attempt to soften it, Sillyboy opened his camera to send Inkdkitty a close-up photograph of the orange Under Armour logo on the hem of his shorts, only to discover *OkCupid* forbids texting images; a humane restriction of function. Sillyboy sat on his mother's psychoanalytic chaise to weather the humiliation, recreating scenarios of romantic failures—some real, others imagined—while refreshing the

OkCupid messaging app for the entire thirty-four minutes it took for Inkdkitty to respond.

Inkdkitty: nice.
wolfewolf: what's your number? Easier to talk that way, yes?
Inkdkitty responded with her number.

Sillyboy texted:

We should smoke sometime
For sure. What's your Facebook? I just need to make sure you're real lol

Still avoiding the rigor of the gym, Sillyboy accepted a friend request from Chloe Addison-Lin; and, in lieu of curls and squats, began to click through hundreds of her photos, beginning with her most recent, featuring Chloe and two female friends posing in bed with a pint of mango ice cream, past photos of parties, road trips, a stint in Europe, foliage and road signs shot on film, boys who may have once been lovers, and culminating in her first album posted: a series of images captured on a primitive digital camera in a high school cafeteria; Chloe's smile gleaming with braces.

Once Sillyboy and Chloe had both investigated each other's Facebook profiles and concluded that neither was being deceived, plans were made to meet over coffee and maybe smoke a joint. Chloe suggested a coffee shop "near her place," a detail underlined in eroticism that leapt from his phone.

It was too hot and humid, even for an August during the epoch in which earth was beginning to implement a feverish cure for its human illness. Sillyboy stepped into his favorite pair of jeans (crotch ripped, repaired, and then ripped once again), slipped on a gray Harley Davidson t-shirt (sleeves gouged so wide his entire flank, and in some positions, even his nipples, were exposed), and slid a used paperback into his back pocket: Phillip Roth's *My Life as a Man*.

Sillyboy was first to arrive at the coffee shop (nipples sliding in and out of view) ablaze with anxiety. He checked his reflection in the window of a parked taxi; its driver on the sidewalk, kneeling on a rectangular rug. Sillyboy sucked in his cheeks and jutted his jaw to experience the rush of serotonin produced by seeing his features momentarily renovated to a more handsome proportional mask. He reveled in his reflection, risking discovery by the driver, who could have finished praying at any moment, and witnessed Sillyboy's embarrassing display of vanity.

Either Chloe was late or Sillyboy was early, and neither was a good sign. Sillyboy pulled out his paperback to appear occupied (idleness being the least sexy sin) and leaned against a streetlamp to read the same sentence, over and over: "As far as I can see, there is no conquering or exorcising the past with words—words born either of imagination or forthrightness."

An eternity passed.

She was taller than he was expecting and a touch broader across the shoulders than she appeared in photos. Sillyboy wondered if she was submissive in bed: if she would fuck his cock with her throat, if she liked her mouth spat into, and if she would swallow? Remembering this was not porn, Sillyboy began to feel self-conscious about his nipples. Sillyboy didn't know if they should shake hands or hug. Chloe, more experienced greeting strangers from the Internet, registered his faltering, and opened her arms to him.

"Have you ever been to D.C?" she asked.

"No, I guess I'm a bad American." Sillyboy answered in the coffee shop.

"That's good," she said, and moved her chair toward the table.

"What do you mean?" Sillyboy said, crossing his legs in the booth.

"Being a bad American is a good thing. Who would want to be a good American? Being a good American means supporting fucked up shit. Guns. Drones. I don't want to get political. I'm apathetic when it comes to politics."

"Yeah."

"Where did you grow up?"

"Manhattan."

"That must've been cool," she said, sipping a chai latte. "Was it?"

"Yeah," he said, smiling, somewhat.

"I'm definitely a suburban girl at heart."

"What does that mean?"

"I guess it means a lot of things. My experiences growing up weren't that good. Whose are?"

"What do you mean?"

"High school was hard for me."

"Why?"

"A lot of reasons."

"Like what?"

"I don't remember much of it. I was so barred out on Xanax I couldn't keep my eyes open."

"Oh. Yeah. Okay."

"It was weird, like..." Chloe trailed off, and the first sign of inhibition appeared on her face.

"What?"

"I am saying too much but whatever. I was just not okay in high school. My boyfriend at the time was also my drug dealer. That's why I was dating him. I mean, he was a hysterical person and still is but, it's whatever, like, I was dating my drug dealer. That's pretty funny."

"It is."

"But it wasn't the smartest move for me."

"Right." Sillyboy tried to laugh.

"But you should know I'm not addicted to drugs anymore. I haven't taken a prescription in over a year."

"That's great," Sillyboy said, modulating his tone to convey what he hoped was an appropriate amount of enthusiasm.

"And the whole reason it started is I needed a way out, you know, like, basically, my parents were pretty abusive."

"How so?"

"In every way. My mother is an alcoholic, emotionally abusive, and manipulative. And my father is a genuinely good person. I adore my father. But he is a traditional Chinese man."

"What does that mean exactly?"

"Physical abuse is a part of being a parent in China and my dad, like, moved to the US when he was thirty, so, he hit me a lot growing up. And I understand it. I do. I understand where he is coming from and, like, honestly, he doesn't love my mother anymore, I am pretty sure, so, I mean, well, he loves her on some level but, like, they are just not a good couple. They should get a divorce but he's too proud. Chinese men are always too proud. The second half of my senior year I didn't live at home. I lived with a friend."

"Why is that?"

"My parents couldn't handle me. Or, like, I couldn't handle them. We would fight constantly, and my dad would hit me because that's what he knows. That's just how he understands how to handle a child who is a problem. So, it was easier for me to live with one of my best friends who's, like, super rich. Pretty sure I went home, like, twice."

"And your parents were cool with that?"

"They were relieved."

"Did they know you were doing drugs?"

"My parents were, and still are, completely clueless. My mother might have suspected but she was too selfish and drunk to care and my father, like, I mean there was a time he literally walked in on me smoking a blunt in my room and he didn't even know. He's smart. He's a genius in his way. But he is deeply naive. He doesn't understand things like drugs. I was angry with them. I wasn't doing well in school, and I was fucked up most of the time, so we fought. I didn't do my schoolwork and we would fight. I would sneak out of my room in the middle of the night to sleep at my boyfriend's house and not be there in the morning, and so when the opportunity came up for me to live somewhere else they were happy, I think. I think they felt it would be easier for another family to deal with me. A family who wasn't my own family."

"Was it easier?"

"Yeah. Much. They just let me do whatever I want. I was still doing everything the same though."

Sillyboy and Chloe sipped their drinks.

"I am telling you all this," Chloe said, breaking the silence, "just ... so you know. Like, I'm not good at lying. I want to be up front with you. This is who I am. It's not my personality to hide who I am."

•

The walls in Chloe's room were covered in many small drawings.

"These are really cool," Sillyboy said, meaning it.

"Thanks, I drew most of them. Some of them I didn't. They're not that good."

"They're good to me."

Chloe sat on her bed underneath a small window without an air conditioning unit. The room had a modest view of a sparsely populated street. She used a thin hard book of sacred geometry to roll them a joint. Sillyboy perched on her desk, deciding when it would be appropriate to sit next to her. They smoked. They talked for a while and became quite stoned. And when he could no longer bear the feeling of not being close to her, he moved cautiously to the bed. After more talking, knees touching now, heat compounding, he asked, gently, if they could kiss.

"Yes," she said, voice small and confident.

For the next three months, as Sillyboy scanned Craigslist for a room in Bushwick, he spent every night in Chloe's bed and succeeded in revealing as little of himself as he did during their first conversation. Sensing Sillyboy's reticence to fill any role other than sexual partner, Chloe filled the time between fucking with her favorite YouTube videos. YouTube was an excellent filler of emotionally ambiguous space and served as insulation, she thought, against a threat always perceived spending time with men met online: sudden disappearance without explanation. Chloe had come to expect disappearance after every text. It was the inverse of violence and yet Chloe experienced it as violent. Chloe experienced herself as at least somewhat cunning whenever she would disappear on a boy. Something had evolved. There seemed to be a new social contract, unwittingly signed by everyone, that to exit a romance required no words. People could simply dispose of others by way of digital silence.

(After more thinking, and a recent bad experience, in which I tried the opposite of a "ghost," and was chastised for my insensitivity and awkwardness; making what should have been a casual fling feel overwrought with unnecessary importance, I wonder now if "ghosting" is humane. Is a "break up" necessary after a handful of encounters? Is the practice of "ghosting" even new? Or, is it evolved language to classify what we have always done with lukewarm feelings: let the unwanted other fade away? Maybe "ghosting" provides a comforting mystery that protects the spurned? And, though publicly much decried, is privately welcomed as insulation around the sting of rejection?)

This was the summer Drake released the album *Nothing was the Same*. Sitting in bed, smoking weed and enjoying all the pleasures of the flesh, Sillyboy and Chloe listened to the album on repeat.

> **Somewhere between psychotic and iconic**
> **Somewhere between I'm sober and I'm lifted**
> **Somewhere between a mistress and commitment.**

Drake and Sillyboy were born in the same year. Eventually, Chloe began to inject their conversations with small doses of intimacy.

"Do you think I'm needy?"

"What do you mean?"

"Guys in the past. Boyfriends, or, like, guys I've dated, some thought I was needy. That's all. I just wanted to know if you feel that way?"

Sillyboy was silent. Chloe, head on his chest, felt his heart rate rise.

"Ah, no. I don't think you're needy."

"That's good."

Over her bed was a sticker that read, "FUCK IT."

"I just don't always live right." Chloe continued.

"In what way?"

"I don't know. It's okay. I probably shouldn't have brought it up."

"Well, you did. So now I am really curious."

"Just like…I don't know. I used to lie to people. I don't really anymore. But I used to lie to people about the weirdest shit that didn't matter."

"Like what?"

"Well, like, when I was in high school, I used to tell people I was adopted, which was so not true. Just little stuff like that."

"That's not that bad. How does that make you a bad person?"

"I don't know. Like, I don't always take the best care of myself."

"In what way specifically?"

"Just, like, you know, bad decisions. Ugh, it's stupid. Teenager stuff. Pretend I never said anything."

To accentuate his pleasure while fucking her, Sillyboy would repeat her age, over and over, ("nineteen"). Like the plummeting price of a stock shorted. Like the price of a priceless item undervalued at a flea market. Sillyboy had to remind himself Chloe was not pornography. The light entering his eyes was not from an image on a screen.

"What are you thinking about?" Chloe asked him as they lay in bed. Sillyboy was thinking about how to become rich and famous. Sillyboy was thinking about becoming anyone other than himself.

"Ah, nothing really. What are you thinking about?"

"Um, I don't know, I'm just wondering why you decided to go on *OkCupid*."

"What do you mean?"

"I don't know, some people go on there just to hook up and then, like, you know, others are actually looking for a relationship."

Sillyboy was silent. Chloe reached for a roach resting

on the lip of an ashtray. She lit, inhaled, and moved it to Sillyboy's mouth where she met his gaze and he glimpsed her pain.

"Um," Sillyboy felt his body disappear into space and wondered how a once-in-a-generation-genius would answer her question. "I don't know what I'm looking for exactly. I guess I was looking for you."

Chloe laughed, secretly ecstatic.

Sillyboy felt her happiness and was frightened.

"I mean, I just moved back to the city," he took a deep breath. "I have no friends here, really. I don't go to bars. It seemed like a good way to meet people."

"Yeah." Chloe nodded on his chest. His heart rate cooled. "So, you never think about falling in love or being in a relationship?" She said, biting the inside corner of her cheek.

"I don't know, I guess... yeah. I guess I'm not really looking for a relationship right now. I need to focus on my work. So, yeah, no. Those aren't things I'm thinking about that much." Chloe kissed him on the mouth with so much romance, as if his words contained their opposite meaning. They made love for the third time that evening. Once again, Sillyboy allowed himself to become mesmerized by her age.

•

Two months later, after finding his own apartment, Sillyboy began to ignore Chloe's invitations to hang out. One night while buying candy at a bodega, he realized he was stringing her along. He decided that to continue to act— physically, at least—as if he were becoming her boyfriend was unkind and must stop.

Still, he didn't text her.

Three nights later, Chloe sent Sillyboy a straightforward text:

You've become pretty distant Sillyboy it's clear to me you aren't interested in this romantically so I think it's best if we don't see each other anymore sorry to be blunt but one of us has to be

Sillyboy was relieved. Chloe had set him free from an uncomfortable arrangement. She was not a profile photo attached to an age on a website he found late at night, horny, but a person in need of love and commitment; both of which he was unprepared to give.

It was winter and the bleak empty streets of Bushwick froze slick with ice. Sillyboy grew lonely. The memory of Chloe glowed warm with nostalgia. Sillyboy's desire to complete a screenplay and become a cinema icon killed his appetite for romance. But the insecurity of this endeavor increased his longing for the surety of Chloe's nineteen and a half-year-old body. A body which allowed him to feel like a teen too, with a lifetime ahead of him to ignore his writing.

•

On a depressed afternoon, as he tried to relax on an uncomfortable couch, scrolling his contacts, he found Chloe's name, and without thinking, texted her a potent word:

Hey

They met at a basement gallery in the East Village where a group of NYU students were exhibiting video art. What Chloe contributed, she never intended to be public: a static shot of a nap, taken with her MacBook, body turned away from the camera; her botched lotus tattoo almost entirely obscured by a comforter heaving and falling with breath. Chloe and Sillyboy were instantly comfortable with each other, as if the first five months of their ambiguous courtship hadn't ended abruptly with a candid text. Sillyboy sincerely liked Chloe's video better than all the others flickering on the grimy water-logged walls of the gallery. Chloe's video, in its obvious lack of effort, communicated something altogether more potent than the others, which brimmed with effort and pretension. Instead, her video functioned, he thought, as a sly satire of the entire event. But Chloe didn't give a shit about video art. Her friend, the curator, simply needed one more video at the last minute, to fill a blank space and Chloe happened to have an unseen project that fit the program. She nodded, smiled, and savored the sweetness of Sillyboy's applause, thrilled that, in his eyes, she was the grand troll of the evening. Chloe excused herself to go to the bathroom, leaving Sillyboy surrounded by art hoes and bros.

The bulb in the bathroom was covered in red gel. The color had a curative effect on the handful of blemishes the winter dryness had aggravated around her mouth. From the sanctuary of the stall, Chloe allowed herself a moment of contentment. It felt good to have Sillyboy text her, enjoy her company, and love her art. They had hung out only a handful of times in public. Just once during the day. Out of the stall, in front of the mirror, Chloe took a close-up photograph of her face, restored by the light, and posted it to Instagram without a caption. Reviewing the photo as it began to accumulate likes, she felt that not only did she look beautiful, but there was finally a discernible quality she could call mature. Gripping her cellphone, she placed the edge to her forehead, shut her eyes, and chanted softly, "be cool, cool, cool, cool."

Chloe walked to where Sillyboy had anchored himself into a circle of people and slid in beside him. It was the second time they touched that night. The place where she pressed her phone swelled with heat. After ten eternal minutes or so, Chloe whispered in his ear that it was time for them to go.

In the subway station, Sillyboy and Chloe waited for the train. Arbitrary statements flew from their mouths. Sillyboy's horniness canceled words of their meaning. Sillyboy was degenerated with desire. He saw Chloe's mouth and imagined a long piece of her labia running between his lips like cured beef. Sillyboy could see only cunt; taste only cunt; hear only cunt in her words; his whole sensory experience inflected by cunt, mouth, and hanging labia: that shy, soft lip, distended gorgeously, one longer than the other, like a rope for the intrepid climber to hoist into the gummy cavern and sleep through the night, warm and protected.

Chloe produced a small egg-shaped-toy from her

backpack and twisted it into halves to reveal a reservoir of tinted lip balm.

"This is all I have." Chloe said. "It's kind of pink."

Sillyboy nodded and Chloe scooped a generous serving of balm onto her lips to transfer the excess onto his.

●

On a queen size blowup mattress in his new apartment —liberated from his mother's couch, fatigued from sex and coming down from cannabis, arms going numb under the weight of body parts—Chloe and Sillyboy began monogamous cohabitation phase two: psychotic love and post-psychotic suffering.

"I'm glad you texted me," she said after a long moment of loud breathing.

"Me too. I've been in here so depressed, like..." His voice trailed off.

"What?"

"Nothing."

"No. What? What were you going to say?"

"It's almost too embarrassing."

"Tell me."

"I was burning this red, like, tarot card candle on one of your drawings."

What!" Her voice was louder than she expected. "What's a red tarot card candle?"

"I really shouldn't be telling you this. It's too embarrassing."

"You have to tell me."

"Do you know Jodorowsky?"

"Who?"

"He's a filmmaker who's into tarot. He's a shaman or, like, yeah, he's a filmmaker who's into spirituality and magic. Anyway, he created his own form of therapy and I've been trying it on myself, I guess."

"What do you mean?"

"You use images from your dreams or objects that contain the spirit of the challenge you're facing. And...I was feeling so depressed about us not being together, I was basically desperate for a way to feel better."

"Aw," Chloe said, moved by his story though it felt like a flimsy piece to hang her entire happiness on.

"I couldn't sleep," he continued, "I was pacing around my room picturing you sad, or I don't know, maybe you were happy, I had no idea how you were feeling. It was maddening. I woke up every morning on fire in the most excruciating misery. So, I bought the Jodorowsky book and one of those candles in the shape of a skull from Catland, burned the candle on top of the drawing you gave me and did my best to meditate or place myself inside of some, like, infinity or whatever. That was the psychomagical act I created for myself. Watching the candle melt on the drawing, not on the drawing, the drawing is fine. It's the glass covering the drawing. The idea was that when the glass was completely covered, I would know how to not feel this terrible. I would either feel resolved or I wouldn't. The drawing, the glass, it's pretty much covered now." Sillyboy motioned toward his desk where Chloe saw her framed drawing covered by a puddle of dry wax once shaped like a skull.

Chloe smiled and felt relieved, even as a low-grade anxiety lingered. There would be no banishing this disquiet. It was the fluid in her barometer; a motivator and watchdog on the lookout for potential misery. Chloe took the joint from Sillyboy who appeared to be thinking.

"Have I told you about my lamps?" he asked.

"Ah, no, I don't think so." Chloe said, confused.

"Well, just to give you an idea of how valuable that lamp is over there, that's a reproduction, but I passed one of these upscale antique shops, like, a month ago and they had the same lamp, an original, so, I asked them how much they were selling it for, and guess how much?"

"I don't know."

"Guess."

"Three thousand dollars?"

Sillyboy laughed and Chloe smacked him hard in the center of the chest.

"Don't make fun of me!"

"Ow! I wasn't!" Sillyboy rubbed the spot where she hit him. "It was one hundred thousand dollars," he said, still rubbing. She turned her head slowly toward the lamp in the corner: thin nickel tubes with three long arms attached to conical shades in black, white, and gray.

"That lamp over there is a hundred thousand dollars?"

"No, no. Not that one. An original. An Arredoluce could get that price. The one I saw in the store was an auction piece. That's a good reproduction. It's the same, basically. Same specs, materials are the same, or similar. But, no, that one, mine, would retail for, like, five or six thousand." Chloe looked at the lamp. She had never been in the presence of such an expensive piece of furniture, and was uncomfortable with how easily Sillyboy discussed the cost of his possessions.

"I love lamps."

"That's nice Silly," she said withholding criticism.

"I know it's kind of lame."

"What is?"

"Lamps. They're dumb. It's dumb to love lamps as much as I do. But I don't know, I'm just saying, it's so nice to be with you. To not be anxious for once and enjoy what's around me."

Chloe looked at him closely, and then away, before speaking. "You know," she said, as a red mark the shape of her hand became visible on his chest. "It could be like this all the time."

"Yeah. It could be. Life should be. Just good." Sillyboy responded.

"Only the best." Chloe said, for the first time.

"Only the best." He responded.

"Only the best!" She said again.

"Only the best!" He responded.

●

"He thinks I'm still a virgin," Chloe said, explaining her dad's stance on sex as they sped past suburbia on a train to their nation's capital to meet her parents.

"How's that possible? Hasn't he met your other boyfriends?" Sillyboy asked.

"Many times. It doesn't matter. To him they're just friends."

Chloe's mom retrieved them from the station in a white Audi sedan and black Chanel blazer and ballerina flats: this would not beat the wealthy allegations. Chloe was rich and Sillyboy was surprised. After listening to Chloe describe her childhood, Sillyboy failed to realize he was imagining her upbringing situated not only in emotional poverty but material poverty as well. A mom slurring her words, a dad removing his belt to issue discipline without discussion were realities so alien to our pampered prince that he placed them in an alien environment: littered with garbage around dilapidated homes, eyes adjusted to scarcity, enormous t-shirts punctured by emaciated limbs.

"They won't let us sleep in the same room, but I'll come downstairs soon as they're asleep and suck your dick," Chloe whispered to Sillyboy before climbing the stairs to her childhood bedroom.

The following evening, at a Mexican restaurant, Chloe sobbed into salsa as she pleaded with her parents to respect her as an artist, while Sillyboy tried to stay neutral, nodding —not too much—revealing nothing.

•

Was it to cleanse themselves of residual trauma, that upon reentry into the City, Chloe and Sillyboy took off on a bender of consumption? Their motives were not clear and they made no effort to discover them. When did the bender begin? Was it returning to Grand Central Station, when in a store for children, Sillyboy clasped a Hello Kitty necklace around Chloe's neck and felt a rush of satisfaction? Or was it witnessing her parent's dissatisfaction at their daughter's aspirations that inspired him to spend his money liberally with the sole purpose of making her happy; to cast her in the role of "spoiled daughter" and himself in the role of "spoiling dad?"

"They don't know me," Chloe said, a dozen times on the train home. "Four simple words" were all she could muster on the subject of her parents.

At first, it pained Chloe to accept the financial inequality in their relationship. She longed to be Sillyboy's equal or at least have the nerve to refuse his generosity and make her biological father proud: to fit the mold of the stubborn Chinese man who accepts nothing. But Chloe soon relaxed into the role of dependent (melted even, an erotic sensation) and when Sillyboy placed his debit card on the bill without itemizing the expenses, Chloe sank even more into him, placed her hand on his thigh, and delighted in the heat coming from his cock. Whatever Chloe wanted in Sillyboy's presence became hers. When, at The Dollar Tree on Knickerbocker, she saw a backpack designed for a baby with the word "SPORTS" enigmatically logoed on the front (Only the Best!); when, from the hulking racks at Beacon's Closet, she mined an original Snoop Dogg *Doggystyle* t-shirt and found the item grossly undervalued; Sillyboy was there to make the purchase, and chant, once again, "Only The Best!

(Oh, how they spent! I watched it all hoping they would eventually share a self-critical laugh, readjust their slogan, and slow their consumption. But their extravagance did not stop!) Sillyboy bought Chloe a winter coat, two pairs of boots, two hamsters named Satan (Satan one and Satan two), marijuana every other day, along with edibles (cookies, chocolates, gummies) all of which added an extra hundred dollars to their usual hundred-and-fifty-dollar expenditure on the plant. Chloe desperately wanted a puppy and Sillyboy considered buying her one—Pitbull or Chihuahua—a dog she promised she would name either Silly, after her boy, or Satan, after her hamsters: all of them dogs, fuck-ups, and devils.

Ultimately, Chloe conceded she was not equipped for the responsibility of parenting a dog (both Satans would prove this true, dying miserably of neglect).

Sillyboy's final gift to Chloe, after which he quietly resolved to spend less, was a premium tattoo-machine handcrafted by the great Ruebendall. The machine was a significant step up for Chloe, whose machine was admittedly "garbage," the cheapest on sale at the tattoo supply store. A poor quality machine made making solid lines even trickier than it was with the best machine. Chloe's new machine would inaugurate a new era of her work and raise her status from amateur to professional. A tool does not the artist make, but a jackhammer is better than a shovel, after all, and Chloe was intent on becoming a master builder.

"This is not a gift," Chloe asserted. "I cannot allow you to buy this for me."

"Why not? I can afford it. It can be a gift."

"No. It's not right. I need to pay for it myself."

"But you need it."

"Yeah, and that's why I will accept this money, but as a loan."

"Okay, baby," he said, swallowing hard, as he

Venmoed her money to PayPal Ruebendall.

"Thank you, daddy," Chloe said, looking at her e-mail.

"You're welcome, baby."

"You my daddy. You know that?"

"Yes, baby. You my little baby. You know that?"

"My big rich daddy."

"Only the best for baby."

"Only the best from daddy."

•

Chloe forgot where she first saw that phrase, but here it is: on August 2, 2014 at 4:30 pm., Chloe ended a call with her father, moments after he demanded, once again, that she give up tattoos, re-enroll in classes, and find a job (janitor was his suggestion, "noble" was one of the adjectives he used) when Chloe, agitated with a familiar anger, allowed herself a handful of spiteful thoughts in the direction of a young woman walking a few paces in front of her, teacup Chihuahua in one hand, bottle of green juice and a collection of shopping bags in the other. Chloe was sure this woman had never suffered the inequity of hearing a father recommend custodial work as a career path. The woman turned onto Prince street and Chloe glimpsed her largest shopping bag where, in bold capital letters, was a bold statement, given the ever-changing landscape of athletic brands:

ADIDAS
ONLY
THE
BEST
FOR
THE
ATHLETE

The End of The Origin of Only the Best!

•

(We return to the present. Chloe and Sillyboi are in their apartment.) Chloe sits with one leg crossed over the other, to expose the place on her ankle where she stenciled "ONLY THE BEST!" for Sillyboi to tattoo. Chloe barks orders at him over the machine's buzz ("not too fast … faster … not too deep … don't stop the line!").

The tattoo is trash. Blown out. Mistake-ridden. An amateurish series of scratches that spell out their motto: a mundane punchline.

Chloe gazes at her new tattoo and smiles beatific.

"It's mad fucked up," Sillyboy says.

"No," Chloe says.

"It is. Look. The lines are crooked. I knew I'd suck."

"I love it."

"Don't lie."

"It's perfect. It's perfectly imperfect."

Sillyboy rolls his eyes. "I guess."

"Shh." Chloe is strict. "Let me love it."

She puts her hands around his neck and kisses him deeply.

"I'm so tired," he says after kissing.

"See!" she says, energetic, "it takes a lot out of you!" They make love and go to sleep, sated, bellies full of sweet notions of certainty. Sillyboi and Chloe sleep soundly even as Nicole blasts Bieber and makes calls, cackling into the early hours of the morning.

FIFTEEN

In the bathroom the next morning, Sillyboi turns on the faucet to convince Chloe he is shitting. He opens Instagram where @celestescott is at the top of his searches, her page unchanged since he checked earlier, in bed, with Chloe asleep next to him. He scans Celeste's photos, looking for a familiar one, on a balcony, arm pointed toward the desert, in a place Sillyboi knows is Palm Springs. The thrill of transgression surges in his blood. He taps Gmail. An invitation appears from the studio that flew him to Los Angeles to play the younger version of the movie star who cannot be named, for Sillyboi and a guest to attend the film's premiere at the Ziegfeld Theater and afterparty at Tavern On The Green. Sillyboi realizes, with a sensation akin to peering over the ledge of a tall building, Celeste will be there, and he must find a way to go without Chloe.

Upon exiting the bathroom and seeing Chloe, at the stove scrambling eggs wearing only his *Dirty Sprite 2* t-shirt, Sillyboi changed his mind. He would avoid the event. It would bring too much disturbance into a relationship that was finally feeling settled after a long period of discontent. *Parties are frivolous and disappointing*, Sillyboi rationalized. He had been to a handful of Hollywood adjacent events, all of which produced nearly fatal insecurity paired dreadfully with the exotic activity of gazing at lives, faces, and talent everyone on Earth envies, loves, and despises in equal measure. Why take another expensive Uber to another gilded hall to feel bland and inferior?

But once the initial shock of the potentially disastrous consequences wore off, Sillyboi realized that to decline the invitation would be an irreparable act of professional self-sabotage. This was the highest profile movie he had ever been in, guaranteed a slot in the canon and to play on thousands of screens: big, small, smaller (on the backside of airplane seats), and smallest (phones). This was an opportunity to exist in the same context as the ultimate fetish object, fame. Not as an anxious outsider but wearing the full body mask of legitimacy, conferred by his grimace as the college-aged version of America's last great movie star. *And Celeste will be there!* He's seen her post from almost every premiere in NYC! Sillyboi has to go, even if it reduces his girlfriend to furious rubble, he must go, and go alone, for a chance to rub shoulders with Celeste!

On the morning of the event, Sillyboi decides to mention it to Chloe. Springing it on her casually would be the best way, he had concluded, to mitigate any discussion surrounding who he might run into, and create a scenario in which Chloe would likely be unavailable. Bringing up the screening at the eleventh hour would make it appear as a clerical error to be brushed aside amidst the rush and swell of the daily grind.

At the coffee shop buying bagels, Chloe offers the cashier a twenty dollar bill to pay for Sillyboi's breakfast.

"Thank you, mommy," Sillyboi says, accepting the everything bagel with cream cheese before asking, in his most effortless thrown-away tone, "Hey, um, what time are you getting off work tonight?"

"Probably close to nine. Same as always. Why?"

"Right, yeah. I was just curious to see if you were getting off earlier."

"No."

"Cool. Okay. Well, I have to go to this screening, like, premiere thing for that movie I'm in."

Chloe is suddenly more alert.

"What movie?"

"Ah, remember, I shot it in Los Angeles? I play the younger version of **[REDACTED]** in college? In a flashback?"

"Oh, yeah, right, lol."

"Lol."

"That's cool. When does it start?"

"Eight. I'm pretty sure. I have to check."

"Oh, that's too bad. I'll have to miss it, baby."

"That's fine, it'll be lame anyway, and I'm not sure I even have a plus one."

"Oh."

"Yeah."

"Is there a party afterwards?"

"Not sure? Maybe? I might not even go. If there is. I'll let you know."

"That's cool, baby."
And the subject is dropped.

SIXTEEN

Everyone in the theater is texting, or perhaps drafting press releases for upcoming projects, glancing from the phone only to determine whether a bona fide celebrity is sitting in the seat directly in front or behind. If someone on the level of Susan Sarandon were discovered close by, hers would be a good name to add to a press release or post. "My Journey As A Plus One Sitting Near Susan Sarandon."

Sillyboi enters the theater—cavernous, coated with crushed red velvet, and filling to capacity with anxious strivers. The first face Sillyboi recognizes belongs to Celeste Scott, who is sitting on the aisle in the central block of seats. Celeste gazes up from her phone at the exact moment Sillyboi enters her line of sight. They make eye contact.

"Celeste!" Sillyboi says in too cheerful a tone.

"Oh my god! Sillyboy!" Celeste says.

They embrace and Sillyboi delights in feeling her small soft breasts against his chest.

"I was hoping you'd be here," Celeste says.

"I am here!" Sillyboi says, laughing nervously.

"So cool. Congratulations!"

"Yeah! So cool! So grateful to be a part of it!" Sillyboi says, suddenly worried that being overly grateful, and not more ruthless and cunning, is the reason he is not yet a major movie star.

"Are you here with Lindsey?" Sillyboi asks, hopefully distracting Celeste from his pathetic display of insecurity masquerading as gratitude. Celeste and Lindsey are good friends. Lindsey plays a small role in Movie X.

"I am." Celeste says cheerfully, before turning to a man in a fitted blue suit typing on a Blackberry.

"Eric!" Celeste shouts. "This is Sillyboy. I told you about him, remember? Sillyboy's a talented actor from New York. Remember we did that indie together in Austin?"

"Of course. Hey man." Eric says, distracted.

Sillyboi shakes Eric's hand, destroyed by the presence of a man in a suit sitting next to his crush.

"Nice to meet you," Eric says.

"Eric's my agent. He also reps Lindsey."

Sillyboi is relieved.

"Are you going to the party afterwards?" Celeste asks.

"Party?"

"Yeah! You're coming right?" Celeste says as Sillyboi notices a dimple in her left cheek and indulges in a quick fantasy in which his bodily fluids accidentally pool there.

"Oh, ah, I didn't realize there was one," Sillyboi says theatrically, both to safeguard against the possibility Chloe has tapped into his phone and is monitoring his every word, and to role play his idea of how the highest status individual would act: ignorant of celebrations, moving effortlessly from event to event, a radiant witness, indifferent.

Celeste looks at him strangely.

"Of course, I'm going!" He says. "Can't wait!"

"Find us after. We have a car. Let's go together."

"Perfect."

Sillyboi walks to the front of the auditorium to a row of unclaimed seats and takes out his phone to fit in with the rest of the crowd. On his home screen is a collection of unread texts from Chloe.

Hi bb. How's the screening?

Did it start?

How late do you think you will be out?

U lied

Are you really not going to respond?

I know you had a plus one and didn't invite me

Panic surges through him. Chloe has opened his email. He's been found out. His only option is to beg for forgiveness or lie.

What are you talking about? Sillyboi texts.

Why didn't you invite me?

The movie is about to start

Is Celeste there?

Chloe please don't do this

I'm really hurt

I didn't have a plus one

You're lying!! I know you have one and I know Celeste is there

Sweetheart I love you I can't talk about this the movie is starting I wish you were here

I CAN'T FUCKING BELIEVE YOU WOULDN'T INVITE ME TO A SCREENING SO YOU COULD BE WITH THAT WHORE

I can't talk about this!!! I'm sorry I didn't have a plus one! I am not lying!

This is really bad Sillyboi

The movie is starting I have to turn my phone off

No you don't

I do

No you don't!!!!!

Call you after wish you were here

•

Outside the theater, amidst throngs of heads swiveling —desperate to catch a glimpse of fame and take their last sip of rarefied air—Sillyboi tilts his chin trying to find Celeste while doing his best to freeze his features into an utterly neutral mask, so that if she were to notice him looking for her, his face would not betray his massive desperation. He pulls out his phone. He has twelve unread texts from Chloe.

"I must find a charger soon," Sillyboi mutters out loud to himself as if later this will make his lie more convincing. "I hope Chloe isn't trying to reach me," he adds for extra effect, the sound of his own voice soothing, bending his reality closer to his fiction. He finds Celeste Scott in his contacts.

"Hello," Celeste answers.

"Hey, it's Sillyboi! Where are you? I don't see you for

some reason."

"In front of the theater. Where are you?"

"Oh damn, I can't hear you."

"In front of the—wait I see you!"

The moment is perfectly tailored to fit Sillyboi's desire. After all the anxious craning of the neck, it is Celeste who notices him, phone held casually from his face at a distance to avoid radiation and signal lack of effort.

Just beyond a group of civilians, relegated to the perimeter by temporary police fencing, is a parked line of Escalades, each flanked by one to three publicists, who alternately check their devices and lists and scan the crowd for clients and others they must chaperone to the afterparty to be present for photographs. In front of the third Escalade, Celeste is smiling and waving next to Lindsey's publicist who moves with the tension common in those working jobs that manage the constant upkeep of the imaginary.

"Who's this?" Lindsey's publicist asks, as Sillyboi lands in front of the hulking vehicle.

"He was in the movie! I said we could give him a ride?" Celeste pleads with all the gravitas and conviction she would use in an audition room reading for DuVernay. The publicist expels a long breath and peers inside the empty Escalade.

"I think...we're full," the publicist says.

"But he was in the movie!" Celeste begs, with even more conviction, as if DuVernay is rooting for her now and all she must do is kill it at the screen test with Joaquin for the studio heads. The publicist clicks sharply through her phone, aggravated by the unexpected request.

"Fine, get in."

Sillyboi and Celeste climb aboard the Escalade and into the back row a moment before it fills to capacity with Lindsey, her parents, her agents, more publicists, a manager, her boyfriend, and an Ecuadorian woman without a plus one —the nanny who raised her. Lindsey, herself, is seated in the passenger's seat, seatbelt off, facing the crowd. Sillyboi feels immediately out of place and sympathizes with the first publicist's instinct to exclude him. A final publicist squeezes into the back row of the car, forcing Sillyboi and Celeste even closer together. Sillyboi's pocket vibrates with a bitter stream of texts. Ten percent battery. He switches his phone to airplane mode to let it die peacefully and quietly of natural causes.

All of the conversation in the Escalade is directed toward the subject of Lindsey's inevitable success in Hollywood. When the Escalade arrives at The Tavern On The Green, Lindsey's parents are sobbing and muttering anecdotes about Lindsey's childhood to whoever will listen.

"I'm gonna make the rounds with Lindsey!" Celeste shouts, as the Escalade arrives, walking quickly away from Sillyboi into the Sturm and Drang of the party. "I'll find you later!"

"Cool, totally," Sillyboi says.

"See you!" Celeste says cheerfully before her features drop comically into a miserable frown.

It's not easy, Sillyboi thinks, seeing sadness on his dear Celeste, *for actors to celebrate each other's success.*

Servers with trays of wine glasses glide past Sillyboi as he stands on the precipice of the party. He takes one and drinks it fast. *Now I can be present,* he thinks, and prowls deeper into the restaurant, looking for the buffet to load himself with garbage food in haute cuisine drag, and wait for an appropriate time to reunite with Celeste.

•

Celeste is sitting on a white leather couch that runs along the perimeter of the main room, drinking from a pint glass filled mostly with ice. She notices Sillyboi, smiles, and confesses the drink is her fourth vodka soda of the evening. So, they are both drunk and Sillyboi hopes their co-drunkenness is a tacit agreement the conversation can begin nearer to desire.

"So where are you living these days?"

"Bushwick."

"With your girlfriend still?"

His answer sticks to the lining of his throat.

"Yeah."

Celeste sheds a layer of tension he had not noticed.

"Cool. Oh, so jealous. I can't wait till I can live in the City. I hate LA, it's so fake. That's such a corny thing to say, of course, but it's true."

"Sure."

"What don't you like about LA?" Celeste asks with genuine interest.

"The ubiquity of the business stresses me out."

"Really? That's it?"

"Yeah."

"I like that. That, actually, is what keeps me on my toes. I love New York so much for the culture, but sometimes I think I would quit being an actor…like, it would feel less urgent to me, or something."

"Yeah, I would probably quit being an actor if I lived in LA."

"No, you wouldn't."

"You're probably right."

"You're such an actor," she says, chewing ice from her drink.

"What's that supposed to mean?"

"So am I."

"That doesn't feel like a compliment."

"Maybe it isn't," Celeste smiles, with a mouthful of ice.

Sillyboi laughs. "Thanks for the neg," he adds, touching his knee to hers.

"Sure…" Celeste is about to say more but stops herself.

"What?"

"Nothing."

"Are you writing right now?" Celeste asks.

"I am."

"Oh, cool, exciting. What?"

"A screenplay. A feature."

"What's it called?"

"*Seventh Grade*."

"Great title."

"Thanks."

"What's it about?"

"It's um…" Considering all the energy Sillyboi put into finding his way to this moment alone with Celeste, it comes as a complete and horrifying surprise to discover the only place his energy should have been applied, and rigorously so, was in contriving an answer to this question on the subject they were bound to discuss, the first question she would likely ask: to explain the plot and ethos of Sillyboi's upcoming masterwork, *Seventh Grade*.

"Oh, shit, ah, I haven't really pitched it, yet."

"That's okay," Celeste says casually, letting him off the hook.

"No. Wait, let me try. Um," Sillyboi looks away from Celeste to remember his artistic intentions. "It's basically an allegory having to do with the tragic absurdity of racism in America."

Celeste looks at him blankly.

"Because, you know, you can't tell the story of one without the story of the other."

"What do you mean?" Celeste asks.

"Racism." Sillyboi says again, sweating, shaking with the sensitivity of the subject.

"Yeah, I know," Celeste says, an edge of defensiveness in her voice.

"Oh sorry, classism is the other thing. Racism and classism. That's what the script is about. No, yeah, sorry, I know you know." Sillyboi is suddenly eager to reveal as little about his script as possible. "Basically, it's a high school movie that's an allegory about racism because I went to high school with some really fucked up racist kids."

Celeste nods, uncomfortable to hear the word "racism" spoken so loudly and so close to her at a business event. She moves her knee an inch away from his.

"But I'm approaching it from a personal place, of

course!" Sillyboi yells to win her back. "It would be ridiculous for me to do it any other way, especially given that," he lowers his voice conspiratorially, "I'm an upper-middle-class white guy who went to private school."

Celeste laughs. "I went to public school!" she exclaims, knees falling back into his, relieved to have a subject other than racism in America to interrogate.

"I went to public school until third grade," Sillyboi says, eager to complicate the record of his privilege with this detail. Celeste must know his upbringing was not all sugar delivered by silver.

"Oh cool," Celeste says.

"So, that's, like, more my mentality."

"What is?"

"The public school mentality."

"Yeah. That makes sense. I don't think I pictured you in private school. I was pretty popular in public school. But it was a charter school, so the education was really great."

"I was definitely an outsider in private school. I was, like, the quintessential outsider."

"What do you mean?"

"I did theater, so that made me really uncool."

Celeste looks at him with a small and practiced expression of concern. "A lot of people feel like outsiders in high school," she says. "If you fit in in high school, you're, like, a loser or a sociopath now."

"Or, really rich, yeah."

"Yeah," she says, eyes lighting up at the idea of massive wealth, or against massive wealth; Sillyboi can't tell.

"Well, that's what my new script is about," he says, hoping to finish on a high note.

"Oh, right!" Celeste says, glancing over her shoulder. "Cool."

"Except I am, like, transposing the feeling I had, the outsider feeling, onto a protagonist who's literally an outsider."

Celeste looks confused.

"Like, I was this Jew in a school full of Jews, so my feeling of outsider-ness was emotional not literal."

Sillyboi realizes he is repeating himself.

"What was emotional?" Celeste asks.

"The feeling I had of, like, being almost mixed race."

"What?" Celeste's eyes go instantly wide with horror. Sillyboi doesn't notice.

"Like, that I was betraying myself. Or, it was, like, I had two identities and I was privileging one to fit in."

"You're mixed race? No, you're not."

Sillyboi looks at Celeste and notices her horror.

"No!" Sillyboi barks, "No! That's, that's not, no. I'm not mixed, no, no, that's, that's, my character. The protagonist of the screenplay I'm working on."

"I'm confused."

"The protagonist of my movie is mixed race. Not me. But that's how I felt almost. You know?"

"No," Celeste says softly, "not really."

Celeste's expression settles into one of low-grade contempt as Sillyboi is struck with the horrifying realization he is saying things, out loud and in public, that sound and are being perceived as racist. Sillyboi is certain he is not racist.

He shakes his head in disbelief. He is on the lookout for Black friends. He will even need a Black friend or two to give him notes on his script when he finally finishes and decides to produce *Seventh Grade*. *I am not racist*, Sillyboi says to himself in a calm intelligent voice he's designed for these moments. *Barack Obama is my favorite president. I voted for Obama twice. I cannot be racist if I want to make movies. Hollywood is the worst place for a person to be racist.*

"Sounds like a cool script," Celeste says. Her expression and body language snap back to neutral.

"Yeah?"

"Race is pretty hot right now. Racism too, I guess," Celeste says, checking her phone.

"Right." Sillyboi says as relief washes over him. "Yeah, no totally, that's, you're so right."

"It sounds like something that could get a grant. Have you thought about applying for one?"

Celeste opens her camera to check her reflection.

"A grant?" Sillyboi says, smiling wide on the inside.

"Have you done any grant writing?" Celeste says, scanning the room.

"No, not yet. Sounds cool though."

Sillyboi sips his chardonnay and finally comprehends Celeste's total lack of interest. The length of time he's been sitting with her suddenly feels extravagant given the probable magnitude of anger at home. Chloe alone, seething, spitting, and considering arson.

"I got to get home actually," Sillyboi announces.

"Okay," Celeste says with a hint of relief.

They stand.

They embrace.

The hug lasts a full moment longer than what is appropriate between friends and as they disengage, his hand lingers on the small of her back. They both feel it: the quaint death rattle of an almost showmance.

SEVENTEEN

The apartment is bright. Sillyboi slips off his dress shoes, doing his best not to disturb the brittle, quiet atmosphere. Chloe shuffles into the living room. Eyes red, shoulders deflated, and presses into him with all her weight.

"Hi," Chloe says into the wool of his jacket.

"Hi."

"You wore your suit?"

"Yeah."

"I like it."

She nuzzles her head into his neck.

"How was the movie?"

"Just okay."

"Were you cute?"

"I guess."

"I'm sorry for the texts."

"It's fine, my phone died."

"Oh."

"Sorry I didn't respond."

"Don't be."

•

When Chloe returns from the bathroom, Sillyboi is in bed, lights off, covers pulled over his head.

"You asleep?" She asks.

Sillyboi throws the covers from his face and smiles. He reaches his arms out and flaps his fingers, beckoning her to join him. She does, and rediscovers how well their bodies fit together. The hours she spent condemning him did nothing to deform him.

"Can I ask you a question?" Sillyboi whispers, grateful she is no longer angry.

"Yes baby."

"Am I ... am I losing my hair?" He asks.

"What?"

"Is my hairline receding?"

"No."

"Really?"

"Do you think it is?"

"I don't know. I've been studying it for the past four or five years and I feel like it's moved back."

Chloe is silent and Sillyboi is gripped by anxiety, as if the small area of space slowly opening at his temples is the stage on which he will reveal all. His deceit. His ineptitude. His interaction with Celeste.

"Have you noticed?" He asks.

"Never."

"Are you sure?"

"Silly. I'm not lying."

"That's good," he says, and remembers his lies.

"You have beautiful hair, baby."

"It's going away," he says, overcome by sadness. "Slowly. Very slowly. It is."

"I don't think you're right," Chloe says.

Sillyboi turns to look in her eyes and see if he can detect any trace of dishonesty.

Chloe smiles, pure and honest.

"I'm glad you think that."

•

In a new restaurant, they sit sipping burnt coffee made palatable by heavy cream. Sillyboi is responding to an email as Chloe's gaze drifts from her phone to the entrance where a man and woman in black leather biker jackets hold on to each other, swaying and dizzy with affection. The woman whispers in the man's ear. He laughs. Chloe glances to Sillyboi staring at his phone. *This is when I must break the silence,* she thinks. *I must be the one to do it. Men can't lift heavy subjects into conversation.*

"Silly?" Her voice is less confident than she was expecting, and her body begins to compress slowly, suffocating her.

"Yeah?" He responds sensing huge unpleasantness on the horizon.

"Can I ask you something?"

"Sure."

"It's not a great subject."

"That's okay." Sillyboi's face freezes.

"Can you be honest with me about something?"

"Of course."

"You aren't going to want to be honest, but I really need you to be, please."

"I'll be honest. What is it?"

"I know you cheated on me."

EPILOGUE

I am alone in my room. I have been here for months. I have not seen or spoken to anyone in a long time. I wake up and write. I have been doing my best to include every detail. I only leave the house when I am too hungry to concentrate. I buy a small container of Sabra hummus and a package of rice crackers made in China. I forget the brand. It doesn't bode well for a brand if the name is not immediately seared in the psyche. I wake up furious with a profound sense of hopelessness and loss. Writing is the only way to soothe the pain and it soothes incompletely. I could not have written as much as I have without my disguise. Especially with events so recent and characters involved still alive and living so close to me. Their proximity feels vaguely threatening.

Last night I dreamt I saw graffiti on a brick wall. It said, "third person = white supremacy." Google confirms this idea doesn't exist. There are no articles or images of the slogan blasted on buildings, protest signs, or posts. The unconscious is inventive and mine provided me with a clear signal to drop the pretense and ditch the affected third person voice of "the narrator." Sillyboy(i) haha. Of course, I had to disguise myself. Today is Easter Sunday. So I am allowing a personal resurrection, of sorts, after so many pages of meaningless talk.

There are two screens in my life. That is all. Two screens make up my existence. I almost made the assertion that one is primary, but this would be incorrect. Each has their function, and each is, in their moment, primary. Right now, my computer screen takes precedence over my phone screen as I am chained to my duty with still more details to set down for posterity. Just now, Chase Bank texted—you see, the primacy of the screens can and will shift in a moment—they suspected a purchase was fraud. It was not. The computer allows me to write and focus on what I consider my work. The phone replaces the computer when I can no longer bear myself and must escape to the world of others as they are transmitted to me via social networking sites. Primarily Instagram. But also, Facebook, and sometimes Twitter. The phone might be more powerful. Instagram is more fun to use on the phone. Instagram is a conduit for lust, jealousy, and wicked attempts at connection. Chloe's activity on that application is all I have of her now. It is the absent pulse I must check—and check constantly—to make sure some weak throb of love is not still lurking.

I tried to count how many times an hour I search her account. That was not a good idea. I don't need another number in my life. I have settled into a predictable routine, back and forth, between writing and her feed. Walking down streets alone, where we once strolled arm in arm, Young Thug in my ears serenading his girl who "got tattoos and piercings," is cruel. It's a cruel God who would release these lyrics to Spotify in the selfsame moment my girl with tattoos and piercings hates me passionately.

From screen to screen. Each new day that passes, the hold my screens have over me grows stronger. I wake gripped by hunger for Instagram. And how many hours pass before I get out of bed and park myself in front of my other screen to consider these words?

I just checked her Instagram again, but, moving forward, it is not in my best interest to detail every time I look. The reader can assume I am constantly looking. I just checked. I broke my promise. Dear reader, in between writing this sentence and the last, I checked. And, I will check again! NOOOOOOO!!!!! NOOOOOOO!!!!!!

Her recent post is two days old, and it exists on her feed like a sliver of glass hidden in the tall fibers of a carpet waiting to pierce my foot. I just watched it again. The post is a close-up video of her drinking a large cup of coffee. Her face, which I often mistook for my own, is now a distant fetish object. Chloe is in the shop. Sitting at the front desk. Music plays. I can't identify the song. Everything she posts feels like a provocation directed at me. Provoking me must be her motivation for posting. She must be aware of my obsession with her content. In the video, Chloe is exhausted, which shows on her fresh face as a pleasant overripeness. She is hungover from a long night of not feeling. Maybe with new friends, or a new boy, or several new boys. God forbid it is just one boy. A new boy to obliterate me. I am preoccupied with the idea of her finding someone. It is basically all I can think about? My only subject. The philanderer waiting, hysterical with grief, to become the thing he despises most: forgotten.

She posts and I investigate every account in the list of likes. This alone takes hours. If I find an account attached to a man she follows, I investigate each of his posts to see which she has liked. This information leads nowhere other than names and faces of men: sentences and images on who they claim to be, who they follow, favorite brands, artists, etc. And I am left to imagine how these men might get inside her perfect holes. A week ago, she made a post I know signals new romance. The photo was taken from a seated position at a card table on the street under scaffolding. The only item visible on the table is a water bottle filled to the cap with cigarette butts. Only one of her knees is visible. Next to her knee is another knee. The two knees are touching. The second knee is in khakis. It belongs to a man.

I have seen this image hundreds, thousands, hundreds of thousands of times and each time I am struck by how it conveys my heartbreak, demeans me to a footnote, taunts me, and leaves everything to my imagination which has now only one engine: Chloe, Chloe, Chloe, Chloe. Why do I hope she is single? I know better than to hope. I learned hope is bad from a book on mindfulness. Hope is the enemy of the present. Avoiding the present must be avoided. Even a present stinging with misery. I want to be present. But walking alone down crowded streets, music loud in my ears, I am not present. I am stuck in the past with Chloe, and my wrongs. I spit bile upward. It rains on my head. Like a whale. Like a guerilla's festive bullets.

I am beautiful, dear reader. It has taken me hundreds of

pages to get to this point, but it is the most important thing I will say. I am gorgeous and sexy. In my youth, I dreamed of being attractive. It was all I wanted out of life. Looking back on photos of myself, from my early teens and adolescence, I can see now I was not a bad looking kid. But I could not recognize it myself. I was completely preoccupied by what I perceived to be imperfections. For years, it was my large nose that troubled me. No, destroyed me. No, took away my entire self with rage. It was too big for my slender face. I was hideous. A disgusting thing no woman could ever want. And yet, people called me handsome, cute, or beautiful even. I did not believe them. I thought they were taunting me. All I wanted was beauty and I did not have it. All I wanted was to be desired, but I was terrified of girls. What would happen if I were to have sex, wouldn't I then become overwhelmed by love?

I was besieged by acne. I woke every morning with new painful explosions littering my face. I was constantly running to reflective surfaces to study the damage. The feeling I associate with that time is similar to one I am experiencing now: constant disappointment. At some point, I forget the context, I began to see through the carpet of scabs and puss and noticed my face had changed. I was suddenly —I had trouble even allowing the thought, terrified of scaring the rarest shyest animal back into the woods— approaching the dream of beauty, of possessing beauty. After months of considering the possible side effects—liver damage, depression, suicide—I took the drug Accutane, a synthetic version of vitamin A, and my pores exploded with a lifetime of puss—but each dose I swallowed increased my happiness tenfold (never was there ever a more potent Prozac)—and my oil glands shrank to size of an infants. Seven months, three doses a day later, my skin was alabaster.

Wearing new skin, I saw a new face. My features developed in all the ways I always prayed they would. Jaw widened to match my long nose, which renovated from bird's beak to statuesque. The bones in my face became definitive planes and my beard matured from disparate smears to an even dusting of divine makeup. I became. I became. My only true moment of becoming. I became beautiful. Oh, how I will fall. How far there is to fall now. I think, gazing at my reflection. So, I fuck and fuck like it's illegal and I am dying. I finally understand why I overuse semicolons (";"). They remind me of pussy. Look, see the gash and the clit.

I am avoiding the present. I have been avoiding the next part since the beginning. I should have started with the end and wrote backward toward the beginning. That would have produced something with a happy ending, at least, which may have been therapeutic during this period of great beauty, misery, and fluttering between screens.

EIGHTEEN

The immediate consequence of Sillyboi admitting to his transgression at SXSW was not the explosion of grief and accusation he had always imagined. Chloe was composed and admitted to fucking a random guy in a lame hardcore band who begged for her number one night at Super Happy. The dual confessions had the balancing constructive effect she had always hoped would visit their relationship in one form or another. And, for a time, they felt pleasantly calm. But winter had only just begun.

It is New Year's Eve and Sillyboi is at his computer doing his best to conceive of a genre-bending second act for *Seventh Grade* when he gets a text from Chloe. Otis, doing his best to avoid drugs that aren't weed, is offering her two doses of Molly procured as a tip from a generous client. Chloe texts Sillyboi with Otis's offer.

Please answer me quickly
Sure let's
You sure you can handle it?
What do you mean?

I don't want you to take it and freak the fuck out
I've done molly before Chloe I love molly
I know you do Sillyboi
Do you?
I don't want to have to deal with you feeling guilty or thinking you're dying or something
I won't
Okay
I can't wait to fuck later
Yeah?
I'm so hard right now thinking about your pussy
I'm so wet thinking about your perfect cock
Can't wait to slide it up inside you later
I want that so badly
Mmm
I'm literally so wet right now I wish you could come fuck me
Me too baby girl. How's your day going?
Okay daddy. How's yours?
Fine
Fine?
Yeah
I am excited to see you later I want to have a nice time tonight I'm sorry for being annoying about the drugs
That's fine baby I adore you

·

Chloe is wearing high-waisted light blue denim slacks and a gray crop top sweater under an extra-large military surplus coat that Sillyboi bought back when their motto was

"Only the Best!" The city is ten degrees warmer than it should be in January. Chloe and Sillyboi make a goofy display of their eye contact as they ingest the chunky yellow crystals of Molly dosed out in pills, clinking the casings like champagne flutes, in the kitchen, as they wait for their Uber. They believe in the promise of a New Year renewal. Their purpose is clear. To achieve renewal. Tonight is their opportunity to leave pain in the past.

Molly digests. They enter the crowded apartment. Chloe is greeted by two old friends from NYU, intimate with her Instagram, gesticulating passionately in the presence of a posting God. *This*, Sillyboi realizes, with a spasm near his heart, *is her first whiff of fame*.

"The skull you did on that wrist!?" Chloe's old friend exclaims.

"You liked it?"

"So lit."

Chloe smiles warm, suddenly comfortable with praise as chemicals flow in her bloodstream. The wattage of the evening increases exponentially and her psyche floods with alarm. Sillyboi wraps his arm around her waist and whispers softly in her ear.

"Oh my god," he says.

"What?"

"I'm so fucking high."

"Me too."

"It's so."

"What?"

"Amazing. Amazing. I love this feeling."

"Me too," Chloe says, but Sillyboi is laughing too loud

to hear. He moves his face to look at her directly.

"You're so beautiful tonight, baby."

"Shut up, Silly." A warm surge of substance flows in her gut and spreads, by way of countless tributaries, into her legs and heart creating an artificial sling of comfort. They relax in hopefulness. They melt into each other. If only they could set up permanent residence in this new place of lightness; hearts locked in the open receiving position. *How is this not the default feeling?* she thinks, as Sillyboi leans in to whisper more, and she wonders if he can finally hear her thoughts and is responding as she always hoped he might.

"I can't hold back from telling you how beautiful you are."

"What?" The crowd is too loud.

"Don't deflect. You're a knockout. You're the most beautiful girl at the party. At any party. I adore you."

"Oh Silly, I love you." Chloe's voice resonates with an ancient timbre and the statement lands in his ear anew.

"I love you," she says again, aware of her new register, and overwhelmed by the feeling that their relationship was utterly shallow till this moment.

"Two minutes!" Someone shouts.

Sillyboi tightens his grip and Chloe feels a rush of euphoria so rich it touches agony.

The room contracts in a single breath.

"Ten, nine, eight, seven..."

Sillyboi whispers again, in her ear, talking fast.

"I love you so fucking much. I can't even believe it. How much I love you. It's insane. I've been looking at you this whole night and I just..." Sillyboi takes a moment to think of the word, "I am so proud. I am so proud to be here with you. I am so fucking proud to be here with you Chloe!" He yells. The crowd counts louder. "I am so lucky! I see this now! I do! I know you think I don't see it! But I have! I always have! This is it! This New Year is the start of something profoundly beautiful for us!"

"Really?" Chloe asks and it hurts.

"Yes!!!!" Sillyboi shouts.

"You mean that?"

"Of course."

"Oh, Sillyboi, don't say that."

"What? Why not?"

"Don't say that if you don't mean it."

"I do!"

"It will make the end so much harder."

"What?! No, don't—"

Cheering interrupts their conversation and they kiss a trillion times more passionately than the others. The pathetic loser others who will evaporate into oblivion. The others who will never taste the delight of genius, let alone, charisma, star-quality, or even commonplace wit. The year is 2016. Obama is president. And the present is disintegrating quickly into the present with comforting illusions mostly maintained.

Back in their apartment, they stumble into the bedroom like a single unit. Chloe needs sex like a signature to guarantee his new lofty claims. Sillyboi has not stopped monologuing on his new and intensified love for Chloe and the sudden miraculous strengthening of their partnership. Sillyboi narrates the evening like the culmination of a fairytale. It is everything Chloe has always wanted to hear.

Chloe and Sillyboi sit on chairs in her office. Justin Bieber's "What Do You Mean" blasts through the walls. Nicole thunders over her stereo.

"HAPPY FUCKING NEW YEARS, NEIGHBORS!!!"

"Silly," Chloe says and looks at her hands resting in her lap. "This may be a dumb question. But you have to tell me, please, I need to know…I know you cheated once in Austin, but…I need to know, before we go further. I'm sorry for asking this now. Were there others?"

"Others how?"

"Other times you cheated?"

"No."

"Silly."

"Yes?"

"Don't lie."

Slowly, he looks at the floor.

"There were."

She is silent.

"How many?"

"I…I don't know."

"A lot?"

"What's a lot?"

"Over five?"

He doubles over, protecting his organs, his softness.

"More than five?"

"No. Probably not, not much, I—"

She starts to cry. "Since we've lived together?" she asks through tears.

"No." He shakes his head. "Not since we've lived

together. No."

"But before?"

He nods.

"So not only just once in Austin?"

He shakes.

"No."

•

They wake up coated in bodily runoff, opponents primed and ready for the fight, nature slicking their surfaces, transforming their edges to sheer rock face, so that each may slip and fall from the other to their death. Chloe rouses Sillyboi from a dreamless sleep with an animal groan and smack on the shoulder. A starter pistol to signal a new era of rage and violence.

"This is not good," she says, voice hoarse from crying, as he remembers last night's conversation and begins to apply words to the wound.

"Baby, please…" He can't go on.

Chloe holds her face, trembling. He hoped sleep would discharge some of her anger but it is born again. Chloe ejects herself from bed and slams the door to the bathroom where she stays for a long time. Out of the bathroom, she walks into her office to apply makeup. He hears deliberate plastic noises. She sighs. He gets out of bed to be present for her. She is dressed in black leggings, a huge black t-shirt, and five times extra-large black hoodie, penciling her eyes with black eyeliner, refusing to look at him.

"I'm going to cry all this off today," she whispers, barely moving her mouth.

"What?"

She is silent.

He takes one step in her direction. She slams her eyebrow pencil on the desk, and thrusts her notebook, headphones, wallet, lighter and pens into her backpack.

"I don't think I've ever seen you get ready this quickly."

She makes a gigantic, nauseated sound and runs past him to snatch her coat and holds it under her arm like their child.

"I don't know why the fuck you think this is an appropriate time for a joke Sillyboi," she says, radiating heat and disgust, "things are really fucked right now. Like, super fucked up. I'm humiliated. I am fucking humiliated by you, and I can't believe you don't realize that."

He opens his mouth.

She is gone. He tries to write. He cannot write a word. He pulls out his phone and checks Instagram. The first post is hers: a screenshot of a caption from Riff Raff's account @jodyhighroller.

Even though I only made 4,000,000 dollars last year and bought the codeine castle I know from the bottom of my Versace soul this year I'm going to double all that because I am cutting everyone out that don't support me! Those who don't want me rich! That don't want me on the covers of magazines! Happy New Year to everyone real! Goodbye to all of you out there who are fake and who hate.

Chloe's caption reads:

Happy New Year to all the real ones! (You know who you are) Posting this because obviously.

Sillyboi throws himself around the apartment, banging his fists on the stove and bouncing on the couch. "Chloe!" he wails through moans. "Chloe! Chloe! What have I done!?" Eyes blurry, he takes in the enormity of her drawings on their walls. He moves his fingers over the paper. He pauses in front of a drawing. A photo-realistic still life of a Motorola Razr, spiked brass knuckles, and a switchblade. Chloe was proud of this work. He turns his head away from the drawing and sobs. The foundation of the building shakes with sobs. Nicole slams on the wall five times and cranks "Hotline Bling" up to eleven as Sillyboi wishes that Chloe were there to witness the scene he is causing.

That evening Chloe is on the couch, stoic, as Sillyboi stumbles around the kitchen crying and pulling his hair, trying to recreate the scene from earlier and doing well, but not that well. He rages to the fridge, opens the freezer, sticks his head in, removes it, and notices a cardboard box on top of the fridge. Inside the box are tools to make a small meal of candy with packages of powder and small molds shaped like burger, hotdog, drumstick and fries. He takes the box and throws it at her feet. She looks at it, silent.

"So, that's it!?" he shouts, "we will never go to China!?"

She is silent. The refrigerator's hum modulates a step up in pitch as it musters more energy to stay cold with the door open.

"I'll get the computer right now and buy tickets! I will pay for us both!" he says.

"Stop," she says.

"I'm serious! Please! Chloe! We have to go now!"

"You have to leave the apartment so I can pack up my things."

"No," he says.

"Leave now."

Sillyboi throws himself at her feet, grabbing her legs, and sobbing into her shins.

"Sillyboi," she says, and kicks her legs free.

"You don't want to go to China?" He says.

She shakes her head.

Wailing gently to himself as if marching to a mass grave, Sillyboi walks to the mountain of shoes by the door, and pulls on black Air Max 95s. Halfway down the stairs his phone vibrates with a text.

Come back

•

Chloe slaps him awake with a flat palm to his chest.

"What the fuck?" He says.

"Get up you piece of shit you have to run errands with me today. I don't trust you alone."

"What are you talking about?"

"I. Do. Not. Trust. You. Alone." Chloe has been awake for hours.

"You fucked her, didn't you?"

"Who?"

"You have to ask who? Is it that many?" She slaps him again. "Wake the fuck up!"

"Chloe please stop!"

"I know you fucked Celeste!! I know you did!!"

"I didn't! Chloe! I didn't! May God strike me down dead! I didn't!

"I can never trust you again. You realize that? You've destroyed my ability to trust anyone!"

"I never even kissed Celeste!"

"You're LYING!"

"I am not!"

She slams her fist hard into his shoulder, gets on top of him, and, using her legs as a vice, holds him in place to deliver a series of slaps and punches to his head, neck, and chest. He pushes her off and pins her arms over her head.

"Don't you dare fucking hit me!" He screams in her face.

"Ow," she says, shocked.

"What?"

"You hurt me."

Chloe starts to cry.

Sillyboi releases her arms.

"You really hurt me!" She says.

•

They walk down Sixth Avenue toward Chinatown. Sillyboi is silent. Chloe is voicing each thought as it arises.

"I thought I was completely psychotic. All of those months. I knew something was going on with you and

Celeste."

"Nothing happened, Chloe."

"That's not true. It did." She takes a moment to consider again. "It did. You went to that party without me. You talked to her about God knows what and something happened. How could it not have happened?"

"Nothing happened!"

She punches him as hard as she can in the arm.

He doesn't react.

"The fact that you could say that is literally all the evidence I need."

They walk a few blocks in silence.

"I don't know how we're going to fix this," she says. "I don't know if it's possible to fix this."

"We can," he says. "That's what we're doing!"

"I asked you, Silly! I asked you! I asked you so many times if there was anything going on between you two and you always said no! You told me I was crazy!"

"I never said you were crazy!"

"You did! You did! You told me I was out of my mind!"

"I never said those words!"

"That's such a mean thing to do! Can you imagine? Seriously, just take a moment to imagine what it would feel like to know something's true, but whenever you bring it up, you're told you're crazy. You're literally told you are out of your mind! That makes a person crazy! I don't know what's worse. I seriously don't. Being cheated on or being made to feel stupid and psychotic."

The next morning eating breakfast at a restaurant, he

experiences the onset of a migraine and can't keep his eyes open or chew. Chloe is calm and reacts with sincere concern. She holds his body, like a wounded soldier and helps him walk home muttering sweet comforts. He shields his eyes from the glaring winter sun. Once in bed, he pulls the comforter over his head. Hours later, he wakes with a text from her.

Are you still in bed?
Yes

His headache has lessened somewhat when she texts again.

How can I trust you?
I am sick
Are you?
Chloe I've been in bed all day asleep
Okay I'll make soup later love you

Careful not to move in any way that might tax his headache, he retrieves his phone from the foot of the bed to call his mother. "This is pathetic," he says out loud, on fire with humiliation, as the phone rings. He doesn't want to call. He wishes he didn't need to. But he has reached the outer limit of his ability. His adult project metastasized with cancer. When his mother answers, he reveals all. The dual admissions. The days of violent fighting. She receives the news as the Freudian does, without judgment. "It sounds like the relationship isn't working," she says. And so, the final push—the permission—comes, at last, as it does, from Mommy.

Chloe walks into the apartment holding shopping bags with materials to make soup. Sillyboi hears groceries drop on the kitchen table and footsteps as she approaches the dark bedroom.

"This relationship isn't working," he says, the moment she enters the room.

Her face contorts in horror.

"Do you love me?" She asks, heaving.

He gazes at a drawing of a rose on their wall.

"I don't know," he says.

She grabs her chest with both hands and moans.

"I loved you so much," she says, as he picks a t-shirt off the floor. "I loved you so much," she says, again.

He hails a cab. He directs the cab to his parent's apartment where he always knew he would escape if the relationship failed.

After putting a pillow and sheets on his mother's couch, she double texts.

If you don't come back this instant we are done Sillyboi
Over forever

He is desperate to text and take it all back. He looks at his phone vibrating with a call from her. He lets it ring. He goes to his parent's bedroom and stares at them sleeping. There is no becoming. No stardom. No beauty. He smashes his phone on the edge of their bed frame, and cracks it open, giving birth to a razor-sharp blade of logic board.

"What's going on?" His father asks, stunned.

"Am I beautiful?" Sillyboi asks, warble-whining like The Joker. "No. I'm not. I'm hideous."

"This behavior is hideous," his mother says, calmly. Sillyboy darkens, gripping his phone. Coming undone. *How could this be happening?* His parents think, after all of the therapy, reading, therapy, reading, therapy, reading, group therapy, and reading coupled with constant careful conscious living, unraveling before them, their precious, precocious, brilliant, Godhead son schizz'd with vanity.

Sillyboi's mother hugs him.

Sillyboi digs the razor-sharp blade of logic board into his mother's neck. A spray of blood blinds him.

Sillyboi's dad makes a brand new noise as he tackles his son. *With the right therapies, the right medications, we can survive this,* Sillyboi imagines his dad thinking as they wrestle to the death on the thick white carpet. *I'll write him in jail. I'll visit once a week. He is still my son. Still my boy. Still my buddy. I'll save his life and mine so we can be happy again.* His mom reaches for her phone but cannot grip with blood slick hands. She gurgles out a tortured breath. His dad untangles himself from their struggle and crawls back to his bride, screaming at her to stay alive. Sillyboi wipes warm blood from his eyes. He sees his dad make an attempt at CPR as his mom turns blue, rattles, and dies. His dad shrieks and attacks him again. *Oedipus*, Sillyboi thinks, thrashing wildly. His dad smashes a fist into the balls his balls made. Howling, Sillyboi leaps backward, into an iron spaniel doorstop near the scrimmage. He grabs the dog and swings, opening a hole in his dad's skull with the dog's tail.

After a few minutes, Sillyboi's balls stop aching. With effort he hauls his dad's body from the floor and arranges it artfully next to his mom.

The second day in his parent's new non-presence, Sillyboi sings numbers from Kander and Ebb's *Cabaret*. He sings "Willkommen." He sings "Two Ladies." He sings "I Don't Care Much." The smell is bad but more palatable in its potency than the ambiguous odor of old age he began to notice, pre-murder, coming from their mouths and pores. Great care is taken to tape trash bags over central air vents and lay towels at the bottom of every door, so the smell doesn't spread to other apartments. After days of performing for his putrid parents, grief comes. They were perfect. They were supportive. They sacrificed with every breath. There is only one way to resolve this injustice: return to the womb. Become again. By the fifth day, his mother's skin is fragile, falling from the bone, perfect for slicing away, which he does, pulling fistfuls of viscera from her stomach to make a small cave in which to climb in and curl up. Sillyboi cuts off his dad's penis—rotten, deflated, raisiny—and positions it on his own stomach as a makeshift umbilical cord so nutrients can flow corpse through corpse into corpse.

(Is this really the end? So, you think daddy and I are impediments to the romantic relationship you crave? Is this a metaphor? Am I supposed to believe Sillyboi has it in him to kill his parents when it takes him years to kill a dysfunctional relationship? What is your obsession with obfuscating allegory? Why not simply write the truth of our life together? Why must you relegate daddy and me to brief one-dimensional mean-spirited subplots? Why not write a novel about how we coach every one of your auditions and how fun, rewarding, and incredibly challenging that is, called *Self Tapes*? Why not write a novel about how we can talk for hours about nearly every aspect of life with so much fluency and joy over breakfast, called *Millet*? Why not write a novel about me, called *Mommy*? Anything but this. Is this "edgy?" I feel this is empty. Our time together is limited. Now is the time for everything to shift. For you to start protecting me. I wanted so much to enjoy this book. And, I did manage to enjoy some of it. But this ending? I don't endorse it. I know I promised I would not interrupt you again; and I rarely allow myself to be this direct when criticizing your work but ...)

He goes to his parent's bedroom and cries at the foot of their bed. They understand what's happened. But what can parents do to mitigate the suffering of their children? Nothing can be forestalled. He tires out as his parents watch.

He takes off his clothing—everything he owns is something Chloe picked out for him—and lies on the couch to sleep for the first time without her, as his body goes into withdrawals from her body. It hurts, not like the migraine did; this is worse, the kind of pain that subsides into history, into biology, that will not yield a proper conclusion.

EPILOGUE CONTINUED

A scarification artist is visiting Super Happy. They carve designs in the skin—Mandala, Buddha, Movie Character (Darth Maul)—and rub them with ink to make pretty scars. This morning I grabbed the smaller screen and searched for her. On her account are two new posts. The first is a close-up of "ONLY THE BEST!" outlined in blue pen. It feels forensic. The next is a video, from the same intimate angle, of a scalpel carving out the skin and scraping it raw. "TEARING THIS TATTOO OUT! FUCK MY EX! LIFE IS LOVE!" is the caption with thousands of likes and hundreds of comments. The audience goes crazy for violence and gore.

ACKNOWLEDGMENTS

Thank you, Shellie Sclan Berman, my 12th grade English teacher for introducing me to literature.

Thank you, Harrison Blackman and Debra Ginsberg, for your sage edits.

Thank you, Betsey Brown, my sister, for being my first reader and editor.

Thank you, Chris Habib, for your artistry that designed the cover.

Thank you, Ron and Jane Brown, my parents, who taught me to follow my bliss.

Thank you, Jon Lindsey and Nathan Dragon, editors and publishers, for believing in this book.

Peter Vack is an actor, filmmaker, and meme admin from New York City. This is his first novel.

Printed in the USA
CPSIA information can be obtained
at www.ICGtesting.com
LVHW041552300624
784350LV00004B/518

9 798990 727519